Midnight Tempest

Midnight Tempest

Midnight Tempest
The Town of Morior
Aurora's Cottage
Lac Noir Lake
The Town of Kinvarra
Trading Post

Midnight Tempest

Copyright 2025 by Kara Douglas

This novel is a work of fiction. All of the names, characters, places, and incidents are the product of the author's imagination. Any resemblance to events, locales, actual persons, living or dead is entirely coincidental.

First Edition 2025

ISBN: 979-8-9885772-7-0

Cover art by @marybegletsova

Map & header art by Charlotte Slegers @charlotteslegers

Art of Nyx & Aurora by @dahrkt

Editing by

Sophie Ramsey | Sophieramsey.edit@gmail.com

Friel Black @greymothediting

Erin Larson | @e.k.b.books

Valon Empire Field Guide

The Fae

Woodland fae
- The Leaders
- Born of the earth
- Territory: Unmarked
- Light manipulation
- Nature & growth
- Healing abilities
- Link to creatures of the land
- Magic gifted from Azmara

Aegis fae
- The Protectors
- Born of blood
- Territory: Drogheda
- Strength
- Control over fire
- Mind manipulation

Skilled in battle & war
Magic gifted from Zillah

Undine Fae
The Defenders of the Sea
Born of the water
Territory: Syreni
Water manipulation
Influence over creatures of the sea
Magic gifted from Xenos

Nocturna "Nox" fae
The Protectors of the Subconscious—Both in Shadows and Dreams
Born of the shadows
Territory: Viridian
Dream influence
Dreamwalkers
Shadow manipulation
Magic gifted from Nyx

* * *

The Divine

Goddesses of the afterlife:

Eurydice
Goddess of the Moon and the Keeper of Souls that make it to Caelum

Vidaris
Goddess of Vengeance and Ruler of the Vale
In the triad of Dark Gods

Lesser Known Gods and Goddesses:

Azmara
    Goddess of Growth and Nature

Nyx
    God of Fear and Dreams
    In the triad of Dark Gods

Zillah
    Goddess of Chaos and War

Astoria
    Goddess of Hope

Xenos
    God of the Seas
    In the triad of Dark Gods

Celeste
    Goddess of Wisdom

Author's Note

This book contains depictions of religious persecution, anxiety, depression, grief, images of blood and gore, death, death of a loved one, and a brief traumatic birth scene. This is not a happily ever after. If any of these may be triggering for you, please read carefully. Feel free to contact the author for further explanation.

For those that find freedom in dreams, and hope within the shadows.

One

Aurora

Aurora always knew she would die within the flames of fire. The vision came to her at a young age, so vivid that she could hear the popping hiss of the inferno as it licked her skin. She never saw more than the blindingly bright flares of light. Heard nothing over the sounds of her own screams.

She didn't know if it would happen to her hundreds of years from now or before she had the chance to fully experience life. Before she would find love or long after she had found someone to share her heart with.

Since she was a little girl, all she was certain of was the flames.

It was why she stayed a healthy distance away from the hearth in her small cottage even now.

She watched her younger brother feeding the small hearth on the far side of the room, their supply of wood dwindling with each passing day. Even with the tight quarters of their rundown home, the fire didn't generate enough warmth to fill the entire cabin. Cold nipped at her cheeks, but she still refused to get any closer.

Her brother stoked the flame, the crackle causing her to inch further away. With his eyes still on his task, he asked her, "Did you change your mind about going to the winter solstice this year?"

Aurora sighed.

Her little brother always thought her to be insane for not going with him to roast sweets in the bonfire or toss in notes of praise to the Divine to signify the start of a new season.

Aurora never explained to him that it wasn't because she *enjoyed* missing out on the merriment, but because every pop and crack of sizzling wood made her flinch. She couldn't stand to be so near the small hearth in her cottage, let alone at a celebration that involved dancing around a roaring bonfire.

Her dream of dying by the flame stuck a fear in her chest she could never quite shake.

"Maybe next time, Max," she said with a knot forming in her throat.

He nodded his head, staring absentmindedly into the hearth. She had never told him of her dream—of the real reason she never went to the solstice. Their family had been through enough after the loss of their parents; she didn't need to worry them further.

"You and Leila will have a lot of fun this year," she added softly.

Aurora knew this wasn't the only solstice she would skip, but Max was still young enough to not push for a reason. He was also never as curious as she, and simply shrugged his shoulders as he continued to build the fire.

"We're almost out of wood." Max had already moved on, his young mind far too in tune with things children shouldn't have to worry about. "Might not last us through the morning. Do you think there's still time left to go gather—"

Bells rang in the distance, a warning of the upcoming curfew, and she silently counted each chime in her head. Ten rings. The two siblings exchanged a glance.

The last thing she needed was for her little brother to venture out past curfew. She'd never forget the *one* time he had accidentally stayed out too late, too young to fully understand the dangers that lurked within the forest.

Aurora and her younger sister were terrified Max had been one of the taken. That he was among the countless villagers who had been disappearing one by one for the last decade. That they would find nothing but his bones a few days after he went missing, just as it had been with all the others.

But she and her sister found him shaking like a leaf beneath a frosted oak tree, his cheeks pink and fingertips bright red from the cold. He was muttering through chattering teeth and blue lips about how he wanted his sisters to awake to a warm cottage for once. He had clutched short sticks to his trembling chest as Aurora sobbed, picturing losing Max to the same darkness they lost their parents to.

She would never let that happen again. For her siblings, she would venture into the wood and feed the hungry flame.

The bells rang out again, nine chimes this time, as the curfew drew closer.

"Get some sleep." Aurora nodded to their shared room. Leila had been fast asleep for hours in one of her own. "I'll be to bed in a bit."

Max rubbed his eyes, the promise of sleep already causing him to brush past her with a sleepy "Good night." He didn't fight her on it, and for that she was grateful. She didn't want him asking why she was staying awake.

Aurora waited until she could hear his soft snores filtering through their thin bedroom door—pausing to do the same at Leila's—before stepping into the wintry night air. It was a cloudless evening, perfect to see the forest floor and search for logs. She would gather enough wood to get them through the night, then set out after the sun rose for a larger supply.

In the morning, she would tell them Maliena stopped by with extra firewood just before midnight had struck and curfew had officially begun. She didn't want to worry them that she had gone out this late, but she wouldn't let them go cold either.

With a final glance at her cottage behind her, she paused one last time, her eyes adjusting to the darkness. No movement came from the front door—no light from oil lamps spilling through the cracked shuttered windows.

Max and Leila were still fast asleep.

She would do anything for her younger brother and sister, but as much as they needed her, she needed them. They were the one thing she had leaned on all these years, certain the gods had abandoned them.

All but *one* god, that is.

Two

Aurora

Snow crunched beneath Aurora's tattered boots, and she focused on the flurries falling around her instead of the plumes of smoke coming from the cottages she passed. They were clustered together, home to fae that had lived there for centuries.

Their homes were boarded up for the night, all shutters closed and doors barred. She didn't fear being caught—no one went out after curfew. No one except for her.

She knew which cottage belonged to each resident, as did everyone who lived in villages this far from the grand palace. They weren't living in a bustling town like Astern, where new fae moved every day. No one moved to this village. Morior was the kind of place where those who were born here hardly left—people here found comfort in normality. Stuck in their ways and their comfortability.

Aurora was among the majority, loving the routine that surrounded this town. But the winter months were times she wished she lived elsewhere. Maybe along the coast of the Andronicus, where the salty air and long, sunny days bled warmth into all seasons.

She buttoned her fur-lined coat to her chin. The snow had stopped, but the temperature was continuing to drop.

Winter was always her least favorite season; the bone-chilling weather put her in a gloomy mood more often than not. Still, there was something beautiful in the harshness of it, like the way the sun reflected off the icy lake that separated her town from the next. Or how icicles would line her cottage's porch, as if nature had decorated for them.

She didn't mind the longer nights, and she certainly didn't mind the bright evening moon as it replaced the sun in the sky. There was something in the night that she always felt closer to, a soothing serenity that permeated the snowy air.

As she neared the opening of the forest, a familiar set of soft blue-gray eyes met hers.

The look in her friend's gaze was one she had given Aurora many times since last winter.

"The bells have already started ringing, Aurora," Maliena said as she stopped in front of her, a freshly hunted rabbit slung over her shoulder. "Are you going back out?"

Aurora considered lying, but Maliena knew her better than that. Her friend saw straight through her before Aurora even tried to speak. Instead, she nodded, biting her lip as she braced herself for Maliena to talk her out of it.

Maliena sighed and shook her head, a few strands from her raven hair falling out of the low knot she had pulled it into. It highlighted her sharp jawline while the moonlight illuminated her deep frown.

"Before you say it, I know it's dangerous," Aurora said quickly. Maliena crossed her arms and raised a brow, adjusting her bow on one shoulder and her rabbit on the other. "I'm just running out for a bit of firewood. I won't stop for any carvings this time."

Maliena watched her closely before her gaze lifted, looking beyond Aurora's shoulder at their quiet, boarded-up town.

"You say that every time," Maliena grumbled. "I should be able to spare a few logs—"

Aurora shook her head quickly, not wanting to take anything from someone who had already helped her family so much. "I'll be back before the final bell," she rushed out.

Her friend shifted her weight from one foot to the other. She opened her mouth to speak, then closed it, hesitating.

"I know I should've planned better," Aurora added, her throat tight.

Maliena let out a breath, gaze softening as she placed a hand on Aurora's shoulder, giving it a light squeeze as she said, "This winter is far harsher than the others since we've been on our own. We're still learning."

Aurora nodded, her muscles tensing as the bells clanged once more.

"Do you want me to come with?" Maliena pressed, her gaze serious. "Two sets of hands are faster than one."

Aurora shifted on her feet, eager to get into the wood. "You should get that rabbit cleaned up and salted. I won't be long."

Maliena nodded.

The truth was, Aurora didn't know for *certain* she would be back before midnight. She didn't want to risk Maliena staying out, too.

"The Lynel girl *and* Gwen's bonded were taken just last week," Maliena reminded her—though she didn't *need* to be reminded. They had talked about the increase in villager disappearances just last night. "Two in one week alone, Aurora!"

She always did this—always tried one way or another to get Aurora to rethink going out—and honestly, Aurora couldn't blame her for trying.

"I'm not *completely* defenseless, Mali," Aurora muttered, though her pulse began to thrum faster at the thought of those who had been taken. "I have my shadows, just like the majority of villagers here."

For good measure, Aurora tugged at the familiar well of magic inside of her, pulling until a tendril of darkness wound its way up her wrists and around her arms. She kicked a small rock on the ground gently, her eyes trained on it as she added, "Besides, he'll protect me."

The curfew bells rang again—seven. Maliena gave her a pointed look and shook her head. "And what if he doesn't this time?"

"Nyx answered my prayer in my time of need," Aurora insisted, shaking off the chill that had seeped into her bones. "That has to count for something."

Maliena's eyes widened, her gaze bouncing around them as she grabbed Aurora's arm and leaned in.

"Don't say his name so close to the village," Maliena whispered fiercely, her brows pinched tightly together. "Even if we are alone out here, you never know who could be lurking nearby."

Aurora swallowed, knowing Maliena was trying to be a good friend.

"Just be careful, okay?" Maliena sighed, her grip loosening. "I know you trust *he* is good, but the rest of the village doesn't see it that way. He's still one of the dark gods."

Nyx being named one of the dark gods was something Aurora had wrestled with every day since last winter. The realm was convinced he was evil, that he hadn't done anything to warrant being worshipped.

But Aurora disagreed.

Six chimes echoed from the center of the village, sending a tingle of anticipation down Aurora's spine.

"I'll be back before the final bell," Aurora promised.

Maliena nodded and gave her a quick hug before leaving Aurora to set off into the darkness of the trees.

Once the village was out of sight behind her, the forest came alive.

Winter-dwelling insects chirped their song, humming staccato rhythms beneath the twinkle of the stars. Glowing butterflies glided through the trees, leaving a dimming light in their wake.

Aurora knew these trees—knew that the moon was rising and the final curfew bell would be ringing soon. But her siblings needed the hearth to stay fed. As dangerous as being out this late was, the elements of harsh, icy nights weren't to be forgotten.

She followed an invisible path into the woods, fresh snow already covering the tracks Maliena had made. It didn't matter how much snow had fallen or how many animal prints crossed over it; she would always know the way into these trees.

Shadows curled around crooked branches, draped over bark as if hanging out to dry. Aurora drifted toward the floating tendrils, her magic purring inside her the closer she got, the magic in the forest mirroring the shadows she possessed within her. She could feel the essence of her people as the dark wisps grazed her cheek, her neck.

It was how she knew not to stray too far from the path. Wandering too far from the wards meant encountering creatures that were best kept away from. The wards had been cast by stronger fae who'd come here to help stave off the dark creatures—beasts with teeth the length of Aurora's long legs, wolves as tall as pine saplings that could run hundreds of paces in a single blink.

Aurora tried to avoid thinking about those creatures as she quickly scavenged the area for firewood. When her arms were nearly full, the final warning bell sounded—one single ring that felt like a death knell, her chest tightening as she hurried her pace.

Her foot caught on a stick, and she tumbled forward, righting herself before she hit the ground as a few pieces of wood toppled out of her grasp. She pressed a palm to her racing heart, huffing a weak laugh at herself.

Aurora adjusted the logs in her arms and cinched the top of her coat tighter. Her breath came out in visible puffs as the moon gleamed above her. She spun around and searched the area for the pieces that had fallen, eager to gather them and hustle back to her cottage.

Her breath caught.

It wasn't a stick or a root she tripped over. A pearly white bone lay on the ground, cleaned so thoroughly that not a speckle of flesh or blood remained. It was too large to be animal—it likely once belonged to a leg.

The Lunar's daughter, close to Aurora's age, had just been announced as missing two days back.

Bile crept up in her throat, and she scrambled away from the bone. Her vision went fuzzy as she bent down to retrieve the fallen wood.

She quickly swiped up the two logs by her feet and didn't stop to pick up any others as she made her way back toward her village. As she trudged through the darkness and snow, images of losing her siblings, of finding *their* bones on the forest floor, plagued her mind.

No one had seen what this darkness was and lived to tell the tale. Even the older fae with gifted magic hadn't been immune to it. Max and Leila wouldn't stand a chance against it.

She took a steadying breath. Her brother and sister were safe, tucked into the warmth of their beds. They would wake up to a warm cottage.

A thick and perfect log caught her eye, nearly back at the start of the forest. She *could* get a few more, enough to warm their breakfast. She couldn't resist grabbing it.

It was past curfew now, the midnight stars gleaming above her, but she didn't feel as much fear as she should. Even as her heart tapped quickly against her chest, a piece of her yearned to stay in the woods just a little longer.

She was close enough to the village that she could see faint outlines of cottages on the outskirts of town.

Aurora peered over her shoulder, the forest dark and quiet. The bone she had stumbled upon should've been enough to send her sprinting back home, but instead her feet turned toward the snowy trees.

This place...it was her only sanctuary to worship the one god she truly wanted to. The one being among the Divine that had answered her prayers in the past.

As her feet carried her back into the wood, flashes of a night she often avoided thinking about surfaced in her memories. The creature that breathed fire charging at her. The prayer she made to the Divine that went unanswered. The desperate plea she made to the dark gods when all of her cries were met with silence.

She touched her collarbone, right where the wispy shadows had curled around her. Shadows that felt out of this realm—so breathtakingly strong, she was nearly consumed by it.

Shadows that could have only belonged to the God of Fear and Dreams, for no other god possessed them.

Nyx had protected her last winter, and he would protect her once again. She believed every word she had said to Maliena. It was the one thought she could hold onto—even if there wasn't truth to it, and she was instead slowly losing her mind, she could at least pretend it was him. The thought of him watching over her made her feel safe— it gave her hope.

And the realm was a dangerous place without hope.

Her pulse quickened as she remembered how he had helped her when no one else had. A gnawing strand of guilt settled low in her stomach as she tried to remember the last time she had properly thanked him for that.

The best she could remember was two weeks ago—far too long for what he had done for her. Aurora had found firewood quick enough; she was already out here. She could spare a few moments for a simple thank-you.

Besides, the final bell had only *just* rung...

With a quick inhale, she spun around, searching for the perfect place to pray to her god. She spotted a wide pine tree just up and to the left. Without wasting another second, she briskly walked to it and stacked her firewood beside its trunk.

She knelt on the forest floor, her pulse pounding.

A familiar raven swooped out of the sky and rested on the branch closest to Aurora. Her lips pulled up slightly at the corners as she waved hello to the bird. It watched her silently in response, its eyes following her movements as they always did.

She was tired of hiding, but her family needed these prayers—

needed Nyx's protection. She would hide as long as she needed to so she could give her thanks to Nyx and pray for continued safety.

He *saved* her that day in the woods last winter, while all the other gods turned away, unconcerned with a mere fae girl from a small village. That was proof enough that he was the only god who might help keep her siblings shielded from the cruelty of their world.

She might not have been seen as worthy of saving to them—she didn't understand why she was to Nyx—but he intervened, anyway. She *knew* it was him. And that was why she risked staying out later tonight, why this wasn't the first time she had done this.

The raven shifted on the branch above her and caused small pieces of ice to crumble off. It watched her as she pulled out a small knife and began to carve into the rough bark.

Nyx, Aurora prayed. *From the stars above to the dirt below, I thank you for watching over me.*

She dug the point of the knife deeper into the tree, chiseling the start of a small star.

I will serve you in any capacity. To keep my family safe, I'll do anything that is asked of me, she continued. *I will not forget how you saved me last winter. Not a day shall pass without thinking of that night—of the answered prayer in my time of need.*

She finished one point of the star and moved on to the next. Her movements were rushed and sloppy, but it was better than nothing.

We need help to find out what monster is plaguing our village, help to figure out how to stop it once and for all. Aurora took a deep breath, her eyes following the blade as she closed another point. *And my siblings—Max and Leila. We need a good trading week, so we can buy new fabrics for winter clothes. Leila's coat is falling apart at the seams and Max's shoes have a hole at the heel.*

Her throat tightened.

Please keep my family safe. Images of them being taken lingered in her mind with each prayer, tainting her thoughts and pressing down on her chest.

She leaned back to admire the star, satisfied with the five points.

Next, she started carving the flames above it, the final markings to complete Nyx's symbol. She would have to cover it up after, hoping it looked like a creature had sharpened its claws on the tree.

I know I'm going to die in a fire one day, but perhaps that day could be a long time from now? She huffed a laugh, devoid of emotion. *Not that you're the keeper of Caelum like Eurydice, or the ruler of dark souls like Vidaris, but if you have any sway over the life of a fae, I would like to live. My siblings need me.*

The raven cawed, and she jumped, her attention pulled back to her surroundings. Insects had stopped singing. Wind rustled thin branches, sending a flurry of snow into the surrounding air.

Nyx, I give thanks for your watchful eye and protection, she prayed and continued to carve. *I give thanks for—*

Her raven cried out from the ground beside her this time, the sound piercing her thoughts and causing her to freeze. That's what it had become: *her* raven. Its wings flapped so close that the tips of its feathers grazed her foot as she looked down at it. It had always perched on a limb above her, never on the forest floor and never this close.

The wind howled around her, sending icy needles piercing her patchy, furred coat. She almost didn't hear the raven's second caw over the roar of the wind, but the bird was relentless, staring up at her. It flapped its wings and cried out again, demanding Aurora's attention.

"What is it?" she whispered.

A chill slid down her neck, trailing the expanse of her spine. She slipped her knife back inside her coat and instead called on her shadows.

The bird hopped closer and fluttered its wings against her knees until she stood.

"Okay, okay." She held her hands up, her brows pulling tightly together.

It was as if it were warning her.

She spun around, moonlight spilling through the trees just

enough to illuminate the forest. A weight pressed against her skin, the teasing of another person nearby. She couldn't see anyone, but she could feel them. The prickling sensation still tapped along her neck, urging her to stay on guard.

A branch cracked behind her, and she whirled, her shadows flaring around her like a shield. While her magic may not have been the strongest, she could still defend herself when needed.

One of the villagers, Elara, stepped from behind a tree, bow in hand. Her wild strawberry-colored hair had been thrown into a messy braid. Curly ringlets had sprung free from the sides, drifting across her face as she adjusted her bowstring.

But what caught Aurora's gaze was the bone she had stumbled over earlier strapped to Elara's belt.

What was Elara doing out here past curfew? There were no guards to keep the villagers in—people didn't venture out past curfew because they *wanted* to. They were terrified of the unnamed beast that haunted their nights.

Aurora slipped to the other side of the oak, staying crouched low to the ground as she pressed her back against the rough bark.

She remained quiet, her heart pounding as she tried to determine if Elara had spotted her. How would she explain kneeling before a tree with a knife—next to Nyx's symbol, no less?

Aurora wasn't a good liar, so she stayed silent until she had no choice but to speak.

Twigs snapped one by one the closer Elara got to the tree.

Suddenly, Aurora's raven flew away, straight toward Elara. The sound of strung animal sinew stretching and wood creaking filled the air. Elara had nocked an arrow.

Aurora peered around the oak just far enough to see Elara shoot at the raven. Her blood thundered in her ears, and an icy freeze spread across her chest. The arrow whizzed paces away from the bird, which safely disappeared into the night sky.

Elara grunted and slung her bow across her shoulder as she turned back toward the tree Aurora was hiding behind. Her eyes were soft, showing no signs of someone who had just caught another villager worshiping one of the dark gods.

Aurora shrank back, reaching for her knife just as a lone howl pierced the air, coming from deeper within the forest in front of her. She heard Elara suck in a sharp breath from behind the trunk, and the sound of her boots padded against the powdery snow, nearing the tree.

Aurora paused as her fingers wrapped around the cold hilt, the snowfall blanketing everything in white and absorbing the sound. If this were any other forest, she would simply be aware of her surroundings, or perhaps grab a bow and arrow like Elara.

But this was no ordinary forest. Even with the curfew in place this last decade, the Cimmerian Forest was not a place to be at night.

She had to do more than just *be aware.*

Being this close to the Zenovia Mountains meant a wolf wasn't always *just* a wolf. A bear wasn't always a bear. Even a fox could have something darker, more sinister lurking beneath its thick white fur.

Still, nothing compared to the monster that plagued their midnights. It was an unknown pit of darkness that surrounded the town of Morior. Villagers had tried to capture the creature, setting up traps or staying awake all hours of the night. But the beast always found a way. Those tasked with taking turns staying awake to guard the town would mysteriously fall asleep, or a small crack in the protective wards would be left unattended.

Aurora didn't want to be out here alone when a hungry creature happened across her. But she didn't want to be caught by Elara either.

She held her breath, waiting to see if Elara was going to investigate the howl—which would lead her to walk right past Aurora's hiding spot.

The footsteps paused from what sounded like just behind her tree, and Aurora's muscles tensed. A beat of silence passed, then a long exhale sounded, Elara's steps fading as she walked back in the direction of the village.

Aurora waited until the forest quieted and her toes had numbed before she moved.

The raven circled back, landing on a low-hanging branch above her.

She turned back to the tree and sent a final prayer.

In my slumber and in my time awake, I am devoted to you.

Her eyes paused briefly over the nearly completed carving, a star with a flame above it. She quickly scratched it out until the image was no longer visible.

The bird flew away from its perch and disappeared into the night.

As she gathered the bundle of wood beside her, she thought of the raven. It had a habit of appearing when she prayed to Nyx—its dark sapphire feathers gleaming in the moonlight while she carved. She found comfort in its presence, wondering if it found comfort in hers, too.

Three

Aurora

The scent of dead fish was already wafting through the trees. Even with the town of Kinvarra being hundreds of paces away from Morior, Aurora could already smell the trading post in Kinvarra's square.

Dread burned in her belly.

Leila chattered beside her, talking about a Woodland girl she liked. Her sister was so joyful. So innocent. And Aurora had almost lost it all last night. Had almost been caught. If she *had* been caught and branded as a traitor, Max and Leila would have been left to fend for themselves.

Elara had been *this close* to finding Aurora hiding behind the tree. She seemed to have been hunting—hunting *what*, Aurora wasn't sure. She could've been looking for the missing Lunar's girl, but then why wouldn't she do that before the final bell?

"It feels like it's going to be a good day," Leila hummed, pulling Aurora from her spiraling thoughts. "Think I'll get something good for us?"

Aurora couldn't stop the smile from overtaking her face if she tried. "I have no doubt," she murmured.

She often spent her mornings showing Leila how to trade their goods for things they needed. And Leila was a fast learner, usually trading up on items that were of far higher value than the thing she had traded them for.

Her sister was clever, fast-witted, and able to talk people into doing things for her. It was how she got Max to do half of her chores one summer until he caught on.

The ground was slick beneath Aurora's feet, and just as she looked over at her sister, her left foot shot out to the side, her body teetering as she slipped. Her arms flung out, balancing herself.

She took a steadying breath and adjusted a few items in her wooden cart, checking to make sure nothing fell out. Her lips tilted down as she inspected the wagon—even if they sold everything, there wouldn't be enough money from sales to put food on the table.

They would have to start rationing food into smaller portions soon if they didn't have a lucky trading day.

When she glanced back at Leila, she found her sister watching her, a look across her face saying she knew what Aurora was thinking.

"You okay, Rora?" Leila whispered, worry creeping into her eyes.

Aurora's chest tightened at the nickname, and she gave a quick nod, her gaze dropping briefly to the cart a final time.

All they had to trade today was two slices of salted goat meat from their small farm, a few bundles of goat cheese wrapped in cloth, and a few bushels of sheep's wool. The sheep's wool would likely get them the most, but there was less of that than everything else. She didn't mind her trips to the trading post, but if they wanted to have a good trade day, they needed more to offer.

With this winter lasting so much longer than the others, their supplies had waned with each passing week that the snow decided to stick around. They couldn't plant or harvest crops with the ground iced over, nor could they buy some from anyone else.

It wasn't just the people who were struggling this season; it was the entire realm. Travelers who came to Kinvarra spoke of the frigid temperatures affecting farms all throughout the land.

Aurora tugged on the wagon's handle and pulled it behind her, only halfway across the frozen water. Lac Noir stretched so wide, she couldn't see the other side while standing on the bank. Not to mention the trees that sprouted up right through the icy lake, their bark spiked and branches bare from surviving frigid winters, making it harder to see across.

"Keep an eye out for the current beneath the ice," Aurora cautioned Leila. "If you can see it moving—"

"Then it's too thin to cross," Leila finished. She poked her stick on the ice before each step, checking the ground before they stepped there. "And always bring a walking stick to poke the ground ahead of you as you walk."

Aurora nodded, her eyes bouncing between checking their path for any weak points—falling into the frozen water beneath was not on her to-do list today—and keeping watch of the forest. The last thing she needed was an animal or beast to smell the meat they had with them and decide it was worth fighting for.

But the Divine must've taken pity on them today, allowing them safe passage without any hiccups.

Once they made it to the other side of the lake, Aurora breathed a soft sigh of relief. It was cold enough that the water was frozen, but not cold enough that there weren't warm patches still.

The old wooden cart squeaked behind her, the back right wheel off-kilter and making the whole cart wobble as they made their way into the village that neighbored theirs.

Aurora settled them into an open space in the center of the trading post. Other sellers gathered in stalls—for those who lived in Kinvarra and built themselves—while the ones that traveled unpacked their wagons.

No sooner after getting settled did a human man approach them, pulling a goat behind him. Leila immediately went to work, the look in her eyes hungry at the possibility of a livestock trade.

The gray-haired man scoffed after Leila finished her sales spiel. "A bushel of sheep's wool isn't a fair trade for a goat." His rounded ears hid beneath a woolen hood.

Aurora had bartered with him this past summer, though he was stubborn and hardly offered anything worth trading. But in this instance, he *was* right. It would take twenty bushels of wool to make exchanging a healthy goat worthwhile.

"Perhaps in the warm season, but the winters here are harsh," Leila said simply. "Have you had a winter this close to the mountains?"

Aurora's gaze swung to the human, curious about his answer. She had just started to see him in the early summer.

The man grunted and looked away.

"This much wool is worth the goat's weight in gold," Leila continued. Her smile was sweet and warm—inviting. Aurora shook her head; she knew Leila's games by now. "You must be cold at night."

His gaze drifted back to her, lowering to the sack of wool in her hand. He nodded his head slowly. Humans had much more to worry about in cold climates than the fae did, and there weren't very many humans this far west. They tended to stick to themselves, settling in their own towns and only going into fae villages for trading.

There was a constant tension between humans and fae, an unsettled feeling of anger that stretched taut when they cohabitated. So, the humans built their own homes—away from the fae.

With her village comprised mostly of fae, Aurora never understood. Even as gossip made its way into town from those who had traveled and returned, she just couldn't comprehend *why*—why there was talk of fae abusing the power they had over humans. Why some humans had turned to dark magic to combat it in return.

With a human king marrying the fae queen, it helped keep fights at bay. But this far west...it was farther from the palace. Farther from the Aegis that helped keep the order. Out here, only the strong survived.

"How about this..." Leila's smile faded as she spoke, her gaze slowly dropping to their wagon. She pulled her braid over her shoulder, playing with the end as she glanced at Aurora and said, "Can we please give him two bushels for the goat, Rora?"

Aurora suppressed a smile. It wasn't her fault if the man didn't know how to barter. "We really shouldn't."

"She gives good milk," the man jumped in. "And she sticks close to wherever you feed her—doesn't wander far."

Aurora hummed and shared a look with Leila as she said, "Just this once."

Leila smiled triumphantly as the man blew out a sigh of relief and handed the goat over. She gave him two bushels of sheep wool—the man none the wiser—and he headed off.

"He's going to be mad when he figures out he got hassled," Aurora said with a shake of her head, amusement dancing in her voice. "Be careful and learn the post before you do that too often."

Leila nodded, a wide smile stretched across her face. "Got us a goat, though."

The goat stuck her nose in the wagon, pushing things around.

It only took until midday for them to trade the rest of their goods—far quicker with Leila here. They managed to get a fresh coat for Leila, but no shoes for Max, just a few leather patches to mend the holes for now. It would have to do.

"Come on, let's get her home before the man comes back." Aurora packed up the wagon, saying her goodbyes to a few people from their town still trading.

"You did well this morning," she said to Leila as they trekked back. "You'll be working in the grove beside the palace before long."

And she meant it; her sister was meant for bigger things. Morior was far too small for her. Leila was brilliant—her mind and her magic. She belonged in a place where her talent could be put to use.

It saddened Aurora to think about Leila leaving one day, because she couldn't imagine herself living anywhere else. Maliena was here; her family was here. She had only ever lived in their cottage. It was home.

All she needed was for the town to accept her belief in Nyx, and she'd be just fine with never leaving.

Aurora pulled her wagon across Lac Noir once more, the sunset splashing shades of violet across the sky, while Leila tugged the goat along.

The moment they made it back to the bank at the edge of their village, the screaming began.

She and Leila exchanged a quick glance, both frozen in place. The hair on Aurora's arms and neck rose as the shrieking continued. Had someone else fallen prey to the beast?

"Go home," she told Leila.

Leila's eyes widened, and the scream faded. "But—"

"*Now,*" Aurora urged. "Tie the goat out back and make sure Max stays inside until I return."

She watched as Leila hustled down the small, worn path to the left of the lake, instead of heading forward into town. The screaming started again, but to Leila's credit, she continued to their cottage without hesitation.

Aurora needed to see what had happened. A part of her was terrified something had happened to Max. She didn't want to voice that fear to Leila and could only pray that Max was there when she returned to their cottage.

Everything in Aurora's body shouted at her to turn around, to go home with Leila and reassure herself that her brother was there, too.

But she couldn't stop her feet from stumbling in the direction of the cries. With a sinking feeling weighing heavy in her gut, she stepped off of the lake.

Four

Aurora

Aurora yanked her cart onto the snowy grass, grunting with frustration as the wheels sank into it. The wagon squeaked behind her as she raced up the hill, her teeth chattering and body trembling with each step she took. By the time she got it up the hill and could see the town's center, her heart sank.

She hurried closer, her breath coming out in small, visible puffs.

Voices rose and fought against one another as she reached the edge of the crowd that had gathered.

"I caught him praying to a dark god," a familiar masculine voice hissed.

Aurora shifted, her face draining of color when she saw it was the town's seamster—a kind and gentle man, his face now twisted in disgust.

"Luca would *never*," another growled back.

No. Not Luca.

Dread squeezed Aurora's chest like a vise.

"Why would Tomlin lie about that?" a woman questioned—it sounded like the seamster's wife.

Aurora pushed forward, finding a figure sprawled out on the snowy street.

Luca—a centuries-old fae who had lived here longer than most of the town.

He was one of the most respected members of the village, someone Aurora's family had turned to for advice more times than she could count. They'd had him over for supper on the last new moon.

Someone near Luca—the crowd too bunched for her to tell who— lifted an object into the air, high enough to see over the people in front of her.

Aurora gripped the handle of the wagon so hard that splinters bit into her skin.

Several townspeople gasped, their horrified expressions turning to hurt as they looked down at Luca.

The crowd shifted, and Aurora pushed closer. A woman came into view, her eyes cast on Luca. Her familiar wild strawberry hair was in the same braid it had been in last night.

What was Elara up to?

In her hand sat a carving—a symbol of the dark gods.

"I saw Luca place this carving beneath our sacred oak just last night," Elara said somberly. There was no joy in her voice at announcing this, no sense of entitlement or smugness. "A part of me didn't want to believe it, but then today Ayliana Lunar's bones turn up? It cannot be a coincidence."

Aurora's eyes widened. She looked around for Ayliana's parents, but they were nowhere to be found. Aurora hadn't told anyone about the bone yet—she didn't know how to explain finding it at such an hour. Besides, there wasn't anything *left* with Elara running off with it.

As much as Aurora wanted to point out that Elara had found the bones *last night*, she rolled her lips together, her mouth staying closed. If she spoke up, she would have to admit when she was out. Then the questions of *why* she was out would follow.

"We cannot tolerate such a blatant display of worship for the triad," Elara pressed, and murmurs of agreement followed half-heartedly.

The town had no leaders, no system by which to follow anyone's orders. But those who found injustice were expected to be the ones to deal out the punishment.

In a town this size, everyone knew everyone. There was hardly a secret that didn't make it out eventually. Still, seeing Luca being pronounced as a triad worshipper was a shock to Aurora. He was the last fae anyone would suspect of worshipping them.

Elara spun around, carving still raised in the air to show the gathering villagers. Some couldn't look at it, while others had tears streaming down their cheeks. They had known Luca just as long as Aurora had—some longer.

The whittled piece of wood displayed three figures: one holding a tree that had been painted orange—Vidaris's burning symbol—another holding a star painted white—Nyx's symbol—and the last wearing a cloak with waves painted onto the back, representing Xenos.

Murmurs about Luca disgracing the sacred oak floated through the town square. To be so bold as to place it there...

Fae were far more superstitious than humans. They were terrified that those who didn't worship Eurydice wouldn't receive her grace, abundance, and protection. She was the keeper of Caelum, the scale that decided which souls deserved to go to their peaceful afterlife or be sentenced to eternal suffering in the Vale. And with the humans mostly congregating in their own settlements, it made for a village filled with little empathy for those who chose to follow the dark gods.

Aurora couldn't help but understand their wariness—their fear. As much as she hated hiding her worship, she knew it was people's fear that drove them to such drastic measures.

She found Maliena in the crowd, their eyes meeting. Maliena

immediately pushed through people, hurriedly walking toward Aurora.

"Do you deny what has been seen?" Elara asked.

Aurora held her breath, her attention turning back to the makeshift trial—though it felt more like an execution. Still, if Luca denied the claims, then there was a chance he could stay. The villagers would all vote after hearing both sides of the story, and the majority would decide his fate. Luca had been a staple in Morior longer than most of the villagers had been alive; he at least had a chance.

But Luca lifted his chin—Aurora's heart sinking as she saw the answer before it left his lips—and said, "I have no interest in lying. I worship all the gods—from Eurydice's light to shine upon us, to asking Celeste to bestow her wisdom, to Xenos, that he may grant us safe passage on the seas, and every god in between."

Aurora's stomach churned, but a flicker of pride stirred along with it. He knew he had a good chance of convincing the town he was innocent, but here he was—confidently proclaiming his beliefs despite knowing the outcome.

As much as Aurora admired his honesty, she knew it wouldn't save him. It didn't matter that he prayed to the other gods too; it mattered that he included the triad in those prayers.

There would be no mercy for him.

"And yet these dark gods are to blame for the lives that have been lost the last decade," a sharp-jawed woman hissed from the crowd. "Why else would Nyx be reported lurking around the outskirt villages?"

Reported being the key word. These were more rumors spreading through the small villages, stories carried to the trading post that made their way back for bedtime stories or fireside tales.

"I saw him standing on the edge of the woods just before curfew last full moon," a woman rushed out—Morganna, Aurora realized. "The same night Marlin disappeared!"

Aurora's jaw tensed. Morganna had once said she rode a dragon. She had also *sworn* Eurydice herself had visited her in her sleep to thank her for being such a dutiful subject. Her account of seeing Nyx didn't hold much weight, and yet the people still reacted. Still flinched and cried out.

"He wants us to be afraid!" another shouted—this time, a small boy. He had lost his parents to the beast just like Aurora had. "The more we fear, the more power he gains."

Aurora shook her head. They had it all wrong—it couldn't be Nyx doing this. Who was to say it wasn't one of Vidaris's creatures that escaped from the Vale?

"Nyx is eating us one by one," someone added, his golden eyes filled with fear. "He *is* the God of Fear and Dreams, after all. He's devouring our terror until there's nothing but bones left. There's never been another creature in texts that can do this. It must be a god!"

Aurora shuddered—she knew they thought Nyx was the beast snatching villagers from their beds at night and leaving their bones in the wood, but it crushed her hope each time she heard it.

By the time Maliena made it to her side, Elara was helping Luca to his feet. His eyes were fixed on the carving, his gaze sad. He knew the price of being caught paying tribute to the dark gods, but he was willing to pay it.

Just as Aurora was.

"Do it," Luca said roughly, his voice hoarse.

The town seemed to hold its breath collectively. Aurora had never seen this done before, but the rumors of the traitor brand circled between villages.

Aurora glanced at Maliena, the two silently conveying the pity they felt for this man. Her stomach twisted as she looked at her friend. As much as Aurora had always understood the villagers' plight and their fear of the dark gods, they *knew* Luca.

He was a good man—a useful part of their society, who would

give his time to help those in need, would spare food when families with small children were lacking. And here they were, casting him off with only tears to spare.

It prickled uneasily beneath the surface of her skin, a hot itching sensation she didn't often feel.

Two broad-chested fae stepped toward Luca, prepared to restrain him. But Luca stuck a hand out to stop them. He slowly shook his head and turned his attention back to Elara. He wasn't going to resist, wouldn't try to run from the pain he was about to feel.

Elara nodded her head once, a quick dip of her chin. She withdrew a short-bladed knife, and Luca closed his eyes.

"One that betrays the Goddess of the Moon by worshiping the Triad of Dark Gods will not eat at our table, nor will they dine with those loyal to her," Elara started. "Luca Anders, you will bear the mark of a traitor so that all may know of your transgression—lest the Goddess of the Moon turn against us for welcoming darkness into our homes. Banishment is the price you pay."

Elara lifted the blade, and the point pressed against Luca's forehead.

Heat erupted in Aurora's chest, the simmering unease now boiling over. It wasn't right. Luca hadn't forsaken the Goddess of the Moon; he was just as devoted to her as anyone else in this village.

Why should he be punished for seeking guidance from all the gods? All to soothe their worry of what Eurydice would do if they allowed him to worship whom he pleased?

They were so afraid of the unknown that they sacrificed anyone who didn't conform. Aurora had always hoped that one day, she would be given the chance to explain how Nyx had answered her prayers. That one day, the Lucas of this village could freely pay tribute to all the gods.

But she saw now how foolish she had been. No one would be willing to listen. Just as no one stood up for Luca now.

Aurora released her tight grip on the wagon's handle and took a step forward.

Maliena's arm shot out, her hand yanking Aurora back as she whispered fiercely, "Remember what happened when Nadia tried to protect her sister from being cast out?" Her gaze was pleading as she added, "You'll be sent out along with him if you try to defend him."

Aurora tried to shrug her off, but Maliena's fingers held firm.

Her friend's gaze bore into Aurora as she said, "Max and Leila need you."

Aurora's body shook, but she didn't fight Maliena anymore. Most who had gathered looked away as Elara carved the cursed mark onto Luca's forehead.

Aurora wanted to look away, but she couldn't tear her gaze from them. Her chest tightened as she watched the ferrum blade—the only element that could stop a fae's healing process—slice into his skin. His jaw clenched as his eyes squeezed shut, but he made no sound— no cries of anguish or screams of pain. She watched as people sobbed but did *nothing* to stop Elara.

Once Elara had finished, there were streaks of crimson staining Luca's face. The face that had smiled at her from across her family's table as she passed a plate of warmed bread to him.

Luca opened his eyes, making no move to wipe away the blood. The mark was a circle with a horizontal line through the middle, signifying the moon being cut in half. He would never be let into another village with this mark, not when the wound would never heal properly.

The scar would remain for the rest of his days, branding him with the symbol of someone who had turned away from Eurydice.

"Gather what you can carry." Elara nodded to his cottage. It was one of the first built in the town, the town Luca had helped *build* from the ground up. "And never return."

Aurora's throat tightened as he stood, his head held high. The crowd parted for him. A sinking realization formed like a heavy pit in her stomach as he left to gather what he could carry. What would Max and Leila do if this were Aurora being banished right now?

She knew the risks each time she prayed to Nyx, but it had been so long since someone was cast out or caught worshipping the dark gods. To see the harsh reality of the lengths people would go to killed what little hope she had of changing their minds.

As Luca's lithe form disappeared down a small path that led to his cottage, her hopes of ever coming out of hiding went along with him.

Five

Aurora

Aurora awoke to the smell of roasting pork, the sizzle of it cooking on an iron slate propelling her out of bed. Her family's cottage was modest, not the largest in the town but by far not the smallest.

She shared sleeping quarters with Max while Leila slept in what used to be their parents' room. Aurora never could fall asleep in there, so she opted to stay with her youngest sibling.

Some cottages in town were composed of one open room, the family squished into a single bed or separated by small cots. She and her siblings at least had their own beds.

Max was already awake, slipping into wool socks that had small holes in the center of the heel. He looked up at Aurora, his mouth turning into a frown.

"Leila rarely roasts meat for breakfast in the winter," he whispered.

He was right—she didn't, not usually until the snow melted. They saved meat for higher trading value at the post when they could. Leila had taken it upon herself to be the cook most days, each of them having their own duties to support each other. Aurora's younger sister wasn't very good with deep conversations, but she had always said that food can soothe the soul.

Aurora nodded and slipped her socks on, too. "Yesterday was a hard day."

Max looked down at the uneven floorboard, his hands twisting in his lap. "Where will Luca go?" he whispered.

Aurora swallowed. An exile hadn't happened since Max was still teething, his days revolving around crying, eating, and babbling. But he had grown up since then, and as much as Aurora wanted to shield her brother from the truth behind what happened to Luca, she knew he was old enough now to understand the punishment.

"Maybe he can stay with us so he doesn't have to be alone," he added, his words rushed as his excitement grew. "I won't tell anyone he's here."

Guilt gnawed at her chest as her brother's wide and hopeful gaze stared up at her. Max was so kind and gentle despite the harshness of his childhood. Even with all they had lost, he was so willing to help someone in need. So willing to make sure Luca wasn't alone.

Just as Aurora had always been taught, she reminded her siblings that as long as they found the stars, they would never be truly alone. Because even through their darkest days, they had each other.

If she were to be taken away from them, what would become of him? A roll of nausea swept through her. Would his childlike gentleness dissolve into harsh bitterness?

"He will always have the stars," she whispered gently. "Remember?"

Max's mouth tilted into a half-smile. "As long as we can find the stars, we will never be alone."

Tears lined Aurora's eyes, and she cleared her throat.

"Luca is smart," she said carefully. "He wouldn't want us to get in trouble by letting him stay here. He's been around much longer than we have. Do you remember the stories he used to tell us of his adventures traveling throughout the realm?"

Max nodded his head, his small brows furrowed as he hung onto Aurora's every word.

"If anyone knows how to take care of themselves, it's him," she whispered. "He'll be okay."

She sent a quick prayer to Nyx to aid in his protection as she gathered Max into a hug. Her little brother clung to her, his slender arms wrapped tightly around her waist. In this moment, she couldn't help but wonder if it wasn't just her siblings she would be hurting if she got caught worshipping Nyx.

Luca may have had stories of traveling for decades throughout the realm, but Aurora had only known Morior. No matter how low their resources got, she always had a sturdy roof over her head and a bed to sleep in.

Could *she* survive out there in the forest if she were to be banished?

Max's stomach grumbled, a loud and gurgling sound that broke the silence coating the room. He laughed, muttering an apology as he unwound himself from the hug.

"Breakfast time?" he asked softly.

Aurora gave him a half-smile, her heart squeezing at the thoughts that plagued her.

Her brother followed her out of their room, the scent of pork, baked bread, and jelly filling the entire cottage.

Leila poked her head from around the corner, her eyes watery. "Breakfast will be ready soon. Set the table, will you, Aurora?" she asked gently, her voice cracking a little at the end. "Max, help me spread the wild berry jelly."

An overwhelming sense of gratitude swept over her. When had it become Leila taking care of Aurora?

She finished arranging the table, thoughts heavy with memories of Luca, just as Max carried the jelly-covered bread over.

Leila shouted out from the other side of the cottage, "Max, can you—"

"Already on it!" Max called back, grabbing the boiling cauldron off a hook over the fire and setting it on the table. Aurora huffed a small laugh at Leila's motherly tone, beginning to wonder who the true eldest sibling was.

Aurora placed tiny satchels of herbs and flowers into the steaming water, letting the tea steep. Her heart warmed; the chill chased away as she watched her siblings bustle around the room. Max stoked the fire, keeping it going to heat the room, while Leila finished bringing the food over.

Even if they didn't have a luxurious breakfast like this each morning, they always had morning tea together. Sometimes oats along with it, or occasionally buttered bread.

The three of them sat around the table, splitting slices of bread and topping them with roasted pork. Max, as the youngest, served everyone herbal tea. Aurora could remember a time when Leila was the youngest and tasked with serving the tea, just old enough to hold the ladle—but that was when more chairs at the table were filled. When their parents were still alive.

Max ladled the tea into each cup, his brows scrunched together in concentration to keep from spilling any on the table.

"May the Goddess of the Moon bring blessings on our day," he recited as he poured Leila's, and recited it once more when he poured Aurora's.

Aurora wasn't certain where the tradition came from—if it was even something the rest of the empire did—but it was a small piece of normalcy she craved today. After seeing Luca branded and cast out yesterday, she hadn't been able to fall asleep last night.

They ate in silence, the air heavy as the sun rose. Rays of light peeked in through the closed shutters, hopefully bringing a brighter day along with it.

"Can we do our lessons beneath the sacred oak today?" Leila asked quietly. "We can pray to Eurydice while we're there."

Aurora's gaze met her sister's, and she knew it went deeper than *just* prayer. What she didn't say aloud was to pray for Luca. Even within the privacy of their cottage, it was better to be safe. People were expected to move on, to shun and not speak of the ones cast out.

"Of course we can."

So, Aurora would ask for Luca to have safe passage to a place he could call home, perhaps even find some happiness.

But she wouldn't be praying to Eurydice.

***

The sacred oak was one of the few trees with leaves still on it in the winter. With every season change, every harsh storm, it remained the same. Its bark was as black as night, while its leaves shone silver. The rumor was that every sacred oak around the realm was a sapling of the Mother Tree—the tree within the palace that housed the history of the empire.

Aurora bent down at the base of its trunk, her knees pressed into the frost-covered grass. She unsheathed her dull blade and hissed as she ran its point across her palm. Beside her, Leila and Max did the same, the tree wide enough for them to spread out around it.

She gazed at the ancient tree, wondering if there was ever a time when the sacred oaks weren't around. Most believed Eurydice herself placed them around the realm as a refuge where her followers could find rest in her presence, but it was more mystery than fact.

They pressed their palms to its bark, offering their blood as a tribute. The icy, jagged surface bit into Aurora's flesh as she whispered prayers meant for Eurydice. Prayers she sent to Nyx instead.

By the time they each said their prayer, their flesh had already knitted back together.

Aurora spread out a blanket beside the oak, the forest around them surprisingly empty this morning. Fae and humans alike from her village and the next over visited this spot, usually filtering in and out at all times of the day.

"Do you think we'll ever get to see the Celestial Temple, Rora?" Leila sighed wistfully. "It must be like being close to Caelum with all those priestesses tending to it. Maybe we would pass by Queen Embry!"

Their sacred oak may not have been as glorious as the Celestial Temple near the palace, with its priestesses and high Sacred holding grand ceremonies, but it was theirs. Maybe one day she would get to see the temple, but she often wondered if it would feel like home as this oak did.

"Maybe one day," Aurora answered with a soft smile.

Max sent a burst of shadows onto the grassy forest floor, and Leila giggled, bringing Aurora's attention back to the lesson she was *supposed* to be teaching.

She didn't mind teaching her siblings most days—she had even come to enjoy it. Their lessons would range from learning how to wield their magic to the history of the empire. Today, it felt like a welcome distraction from the weight of Luca's exile.

"You're supposed to be accessing your dream realm, Leila," Aurora scolded lightly. "Go on."

Leila coughed, a poor attempt to cover her fading giggle as she lay down on the blanket.

"Remember, you're to stay asleep and dreamwalk through the waking realm," Aurora reminded her, her voice softer. "I want you to tell me what I wrote on the ground behind me."

"You're so much better at it than I am," Leila said with a sigh.

Aurora huffed a laugh and said, "I'm older. You'll get there soon."

Actually, Leila excelled at it—so much so that Aurora struggled to teach her new things. The moment she realized how talented her younger sister was, she made it her mission to teach her everything she knew.

Aurora knew Leila would soon be good enough to be considered for a position tending to the dream orbs closer to the palace. And what more could she want for her adventurous, free-spirited sibling? Even if the thought of her leaving sent an ache through her chest.

Leila groaned but kept her eyes closed. She wiggled against the blanket and closed her eyes. Soon, her breathing evened out, and her chest slowly rose and fell. She would be going into their dream realm and breaking through to the waking realm while her body still slept, allowing her mind to wander free. She didn't have to go far, just far enough to see what Aurora had written in the dirt.

Once Aurora was certain her sister was asleep, she twisted around and scribbled a phrase into the ground, her fingertip going numb in the icy soil.

Max twirled shadows around a finger, while his other hand rested under his chin. He was the picture of boredom. His skill came as shadow magic, not dreamwalking. While all Nocturna fae could influence dreams, not all could move around in the waking realm while asleep. They were different from the other fae in that regard, their magic extending from the corporeal realm and into the veil just behind it.

His mouth popped open, but Aurora placed a finger over her lips, motioning for him to keep quiet. The last thing she wanted was for Leila to wake back up and have to start all over again.

Max continued practicing, calling on his shadows and reining them back in until Leila's eyes popped open. She smiled and whispered, "'Fly on the wings of a raven.'"

Aurora smiled back and nodded her head. She had written *Fly on the wings of a raven* in the dirt behind her.

"Let's call it a day," Aurora suggested. "We can rest here and pray for a bit before going home."

Max groaned, but Leila readily agreed. Her sister understood the importance of giving thanks to the beings that created them, but Max hadn't quite found enjoyment in it yet.

They spent the rest of the afternoon beneath the sacred oak, occasionally praying in silence in each other's company or chatting about everything under the sun.

On the walk back to their cottage, they stopped by Maliena's home to visit, and Max begged them to stop and see a human girl he was infatuated with.

Each sibling completed their chores and helped prepare for dinner, all while Aurora couldn't help but think how lucky she was to have them. She wished Luca had a family. Maybe if he weren't alone here, he wouldn't have had to be cast out.

As Aurora climbed into bed that night, her thoughts remained plagued by him. She wondered where he was now and how he would survive alone in the forest. It haunted her thoughts as she tried to fall asleep, but even as Max's little snores filled the room, she couldn't seem to find sleep.

She rolled onto her back and stared up at the planked ceiling. She took a deep breath in and tugged on her Essence, pulling her magic from within her and releasing it as she blew out a breath.

Dark tendrils filled the ceiling, dancing along the planks and curling into the corners. She watched the shadows, moving them around to pass the time. The magic within her hummed in excitement, and she formed the wisps into a shadowy raven. It flew around the room, a caged bird with nowhere to go.

Her eyes grew heavy, but not enough to drift into sleep. She kept the bird flying above her, glancing at Max to make sure he was still asleep. His eyes were closed, his arms wrapped around a stuffed wolf that Mother had sewn for him.

Aurora rolled over so that her back was to him, careful to move slowly. She reached between the bed and the wall, fingers grasping for the corner of a loose board. Her pinky caught on a plank that was slightly raised, and she smiled.

The sound of the other bed creaking made her snatch her hand up. Her heart started beating wildly, and she waited ten breaths before moving. She glanced over her shoulder to see that Max had turned over, his back to her now. She released a breath and reached back down to the floorboard against the wall, lifting the loose wood until she could find what she was looking for.

Her hand wrapped around a singular wooden carving, small enough to fit in her palm.

Quietly, she slipped it under her pillow, the tension in her chest easing instantly. The raven still flew above her, but the shadows were growing weaker as her eyes became heavier.

Her thumb traced the carving that she knew so well: a five-pointed star. It wasn't painted white and wasn't being held by a figure like Luca's was. She could likely explain it away as a project she was working on for the solstice if it were found.

But in her heart, she knew. This was Nyx's symbol.

An echo of her mother's laugh bounced around the room as she gripped onto the star.

Aurora drifted in and out of sleep, her dreams a memory of the past. A memory of her mother placing the wooden carving in her hand, wrapping her small fingers around it as she told her, *"As long as you have the stars, you will never truly be alone, my darling."*

Aurora's body relaxed, but her fingers remained wrapped around the star. She fell asleep, sending thoughts of luck and safety for Luca to Nyx. It may not have been a proper prayer without paying tribute, but it lulled her to sleep, regardless.

She dreamt of a midnight-feathered raven for a single hour of peace.

Six

Aurora

The next day was much the same for Aurora—taking Leila to the trading post in Kinvarra, lessons with her and Max in the afternoon, then chores and dinner.

Maliena had joined them for the night, bringing over honey and fresh bread. She stayed behind to help clean, even after Leila and Max had gone to bed.

But Aurora still couldn't think about much other than how Luca was doing. She saw images of him huddled beside a small fire to keep warm. Imagined him finding a cave to take cover in on snowy nights and shivering as the temperature dropped with the sun.

Perhaps he would find a way to build himself a small cottage—solitary but safe.

Then there were the darker thoughts. The less hopeful. The ones that forced their way into her mind no matter how hard she tried to push them away. Thoughts of beasts waiting for Luca to fall asleep in the cave so they could pounce as he slept. Or of the days he wasn't successful in hunting game, his belly empty for nights on end.

No matter what Aurora did, she couldn't shake the thought that she could've done *something*. She was just as guilty as he was when it came to worshipping a dark god, and yet here she sat. Safe and fed in her warm cottage.

And there was no end in sight to a realm where it would be accepted to pray to Nyx. What happened to Luca could've just as easily happened to her.

"You're awfully quiet tonight," Maliena said as she washed the plates with cold well water. "Something on your mind?"

Her voice hinted that she already *knew* what was on Aurora's mind, but she answered her anyway.

"What happened to Luca..." Aurora's throat closed, the unsaid words hanging in the air.

Maliena carefully set the plate in her hand down and turned to face Aurora fully as she guessed, "Could happen to you?"

Aurora nodded, wrapping her arms around herself. "Luca was just doing what he believed in." She sighed heavily, drying the plate Maliena had just finished washing. "Something has to change. People are scared enough with this *thing* snatching villagers up at night. They shouldn't be afraid to worship who they want to as well."

Maliena's eyes shone with unshed tears. She didn't respond, giving Aurora time to get it all out.

There was a time everyone could pray to all the gods openly, or so her mother had said. Aurora had never experienced that, but her mother told her stories of growing up where villagers would pay tribute to *all* of the Divine.

Now, no one dared to pray to the triad unless they were willing to go through what Luca had. At least in Morior, that's how it was. It made Aurora wonder if the entire realm was that way—even though she had been told it was, she hadn't seen it with her own eyes.

As much as her pulse picked up at the thought of finding out how true those rumors were, she couldn't uproot Leila and Max's lives. And besides, this was her home. This was where her father had built their cottage—where her mother carved small lines to track her and her siblings' heights in the kitchen.

If she left, how would she stay connected to them?

A crushing weight settled against her chest, weighing her down. She couldn't leave—didn't *want* to leave. But she couldn't stop praying to Nyx either. Even with her being able to pray safely within the confines of her mind, what kind of person did that make her?

As frightened as she was to be caught, she wouldn't let that fear rule her life.

Aurora lowered her voice and added, "It's hard to just...*stop* worshipping him, Mali. It feels like betraying every instinct inside of me to not do it." She closed her eyes briefly, a single tear sliding down her cheek before she continued. "But Max and Leila need me. I can't risk it."

Maliena stepped forward, placing her hands on Aurora's shoulders as she held her gaze. "Don't you see all that you've done for them—all that you've sacrificed?" she urged. "I'm not saying to be careless, but for just a moment, consider what you've done for them this past decade.

"You grew up faster than any child should, and you leaned on members of our community in that first year so you would do right by your siblings," she said firmly. "Max and Leila were helpless for a time, but Aurora, can't you see how they've grown? Look at Leila— you've taught her how to haggle at the market better than any of us.

"Not to mention how you've taught her how to ration, store, and cook a meal." Maliena smiled sadly. "And Max, who can not only start a fire, but knows how to keep it burning without wasting too much wood."

Aurora looked away from her friend, the intensity in her gaze too much to bear.

She knew these things about them—had sat while Leila refused to accept her help in the kitchen. Had stood at a distance as Max built a fire in their hearth.

"I'm not saying they don't need you. Of course they still do," Maliena said gently, and Aurora looked back at her. There was nothing but compassion shining in her eyes. "But don't be afraid to do something for yourself, too. I want you to be careful, but I don't want you to deny what your soul craves for in spite of it. People spend too much time being afraid to do what their heart desires."

Maliena's words slowly sank into Aurora's chest, like rain saturating the dry and cracked soil. A whir of emotions spun through her, a war within her mind between wanting to do the safe thing by not worshipping Nyx and being brave like Maliena said.

Was it truly not so black and white? She had spent the past year fighting the urge to pay tribute to him—failing on more than several occasions. Maybe there *could* be a day when the villagers realized Nyx wasn't the enemy.

Her heart pounded in her chest as the idea began to take form.

There was one thing that would convince them he wasn't as evil as they might think. If she proved he wasn't the one responsible for the disappearing villagers, perhaps it would give her—give everyone—the chance to openly worship him.

She didn't even know if there were others in the town that felt the way she did. All she knew was that no one would've suspected Luca of such a thing, and yet there he was, praying to each and every god among the Divine.

"There still may be a day Eurydice answers us," Maliena whispered hopefully. She was among the majority of the empire that still prayed to the Goddess of the Moon, keeper of Caelum and guide to the souls who passed over into its light.

But not Aurora.

She glanced up at the moon, its light hidden through the snow-topped trees. "And where was Eurydice when the ignavis attacked me last winter?" she asked, her lungs squeezing at the thought of the horrifying creature. "I prayed to every god—Azmara, Celeste, Astoria, *Eurydice*. None of them answered."

None except Nyx.

Aurora had been certain she would not have walked out of the wood that night. But she *did*. She was living, breathing proof that *one* god had answered her plea.

"I know," Maliena breathed. "Goddess, I wish you had let me go out with you that night."

Aurora swallowed. If Maliena had gone with her, then the ignavis might not have ever attacked. And if it never attacked, then she never would have seen proof of how Nyx cared for those who were loyal to him.

Her gaze flickered over to the hearth, mind wandering as she watched the embers crackle off of it. She could practically see its wings in the fire, taunting her with memories of the past.

The ignavis had been small—similar to the size and shape of a falcon—but it was so fast she had no chance of outrunning it. These particular creatures burned their prey before they ate them, charring them until the life had been drained out of them entirely.

With a vision showing her death coming by fire, she had been *terrified*. Too far from her village, she hadn't kept track of her steps while gathering wild berries. She'd fought off the ignavis as long as she could, her shadows slowly draining and her legs wobbly. Every prayer she sent to the gods was answered in silence.

Until a chain of shadows wrapped around the beast's neck and held it down long enough for her to get away. A raven had landed beside her, watching as she raced away. Once she was safely at the edge of the woods, her village in sight, she heard the wailing of a creature being strangled until the cries abruptly cut off.

She'd almost convinced herself it had been remnants of the wards protecting her somehow, even beyond the village, or a hidden fae helping. But that night, she dreamt of Nyx. She didn't see his face or hear his voice, but she saw his eyes—one midnight-blue and the other bright green. Every text in history spoke of split irises, but even without that, she just...*knew*.

Something deep inside of her hummed to life in that dream. Perhaps it was that Nyx gifted Nocturna fae shadows that made her feel his presence. Either way, she knew he had saved her that night in the forest.

A pop crackled from the hearth, and Aurora jumped, tearing her gaze away from the flames. She cleared her throat, her eyes rimmed with unshed tears.

"I wasn't alone that night," she rasped, her throat as raw as the emotions she displayed. "Nyx was with me."

Maliena hummed and said, "You're always so certain it was him."

Aurora never knew for certain if Maliena believed her story about Nyx saving her, though she often leaned toward the skeptical side of things. No matter what, Maliena had been there for her and her siblings more than anyone else in the village.

But still, Aurora *was* certain.

She saw his eyes in her dreams, the ones described throughout texts for millennia. Aurora didn't have much left of her mother, but she had the strength of her belief in the God of Fear and Dreams.

The memory of her mother sweeping their cottage and humming songs of prayers to Nyx filtered into her mind. As clear as if her mother were standing in front of her, her words played within her thoughts. *"Nyx gifted us shadows, Aurora. We mustn't forget how good he's been to us, even if others do. If all we have left is faith, then we are left with riches."*

"It's called faith, Mali," Aurora whispered softly, her chest warming at the thought of it. "I had it the day he saved me from the ignavis, and I've had it every day since."

Her friend looked away, gaze cast toward the ground as she let out a soft sigh. When she looked back up, Aurora could see the warning shining in her eyes before the words left her mouth.

"Just...be careful, Rora," Maliena said slowly. "You have every right to worship who you want, but Nyx is in the triad for a *reason*. Xenos may be the God of the Seas, but he's more unpredictable than the current. Vidaris will always be the Goddess of Vengeance, and Nyx will always be the God of Fear and Dreams," she added quietly, her eyes soft and words gentle. "Unless he stops being the fear part, I doubt he would be accepted as anything other than dark."

Aurora hated that the realm saw things so black and white. What about the grays? The violets and golds? But the line had been drawn in the sand with the Triad of Dark Gods. All the fae had labeled them as *evil* for centuries—the Woodlands, whose magic flowed through trees and crops; the Undine, who lived among the depths of the Andronicus Sea; and *especially* the Aegis, bred for war and chaos. But what bothered her more than anything was that the Nocturna fae, *her people*, turned against the very god that created them.

"But he *isn't* dark, Mali," Aurora huffed, her frustration aimed at the surrounding realm. "How can he be dark if he saved me?"

Maliena fell quiet. They had engaged in this same conversation time and time again.

"I doubt the rest of the empire would see it that way," Maliena whispered. "Half the village still thinks the monster terrorizing us is Nyx himself."

It wasn't fair. Aurora wanted to tell everyone what he had done for her, but she knew no one would listen—rather, they would likely cast her out simply for believing in one of the dark gods.

He *couldn't* be the beast killing villagers. Maybe it was blind hope or foolish trust, but whatever it was, Aurora didn't believe he would do it.

"Why would he save me from the ignavis but kill the rest of the town?" Aurora pressed.

Maliena's brow furrowed. Neither of them had a real answer.

"Look, I trust you," Maliena said with a sigh. "If you want to pay tribute to Nyx, you should be allowed to do that without fear of being exiled. You aren't praying to Vidaris or offering yourself to her darkness. Nyx has been fairly neutral, all things considered."

Aurora smiled at her, knowing that Maliena might not have understood her belief in Nyx, but she was at least willing to *try* to see where she was coming from. It was more than most people would do when it came to the God of Fear and Dreams.

"All things considered," Aurora repeated softly. She swallowed the lump in her throat, her emotions rising to the surface. "Not everyone sees it that way."

Maliena nodded slowly. "*But* you're lucky I don't believe the town's gossip."

Her friend helped her finish up in the kitchen before setting off with a quick hug and goodbye.

As Aurora lay in bed that night, she wondered how Maliena had so much hope in a goddess that was so silent.

She drifted into sleep, her hand clasped tightly around her wooden star.

The moment she awoke within her dream realm, she felt the veil of alertness drape across her mind like a warm, cozy blanket. Her limbs moved in a slow, weighed-down motion, as if she were wading through thick water as she gained her bearings.

Her dreams took her back to the forest, the caw of her raven echoing through the trees followed by the flapping of wings. Only she didn't see it. Darkness enveloped the wood and clouds covered the moon's shine.

She hadn't meant to dreamwalk tonight, but she found herself here, regardless. Her dreams differed from when she was awake, her limbs slightly heavier and slower. It was always this way when she was dreamwalking—like she was stuck in the in-between while the waking realm continued on.

She may not have been able to dreamwalk very far from her physical body, but it was enough to make her feel a sense of freedom here more than anywhere else. It was one of her favorite things about being a Nocturna fae—the idea of her spirit being anywhere while her body lay safely in her bed. It was like having a secret room only she had access to.

"You should be far more careful, Aurora," a deep voice hummed against her ear.

She gasped and spun toward the voice, only to find the forest empty around her.

"Who's there?" Her hands began to shake. There was no hiding the fear that she felt.

She was in control of her dreams, and there *shouldn't* be anyone else here. But that didn't stop dark creatures that fed on the dreams of Nocturna fae from slipping in through small cracks in her mind.

Her hands trembled as the sound of boots pressing into the snow came closer. She took a step back, her body bumping into the rough bark of a slender pine tree.

"Though I do appreciate your tenacity." The voice came from her left, but the forest was too dark for her to see through the trees. "Perhaps you shouldn't risk it so openly."

Through the darkness, a figure took form.

The outline of his angular jawline was sharp in the moonlight. Her breath came in small pants, and she briefly wondered if the vision she had of her death by flames was truly just a dream. Maybe this was how she met her grave—a monster devouring her in her sleep.

The figure continued toward her, his movements fluid as if he were walking on air. The coat he wore stretched down to his knees and rustled against the wind; small pieces of something stitched together covered it. She squinted as the fabric took form—not fabric. Raven feathers.

At first glance, he seemed to be fae, with ears that formed a sharp point—unlike humans with their curved, round shape—a height that towered over her so that she had to tilt her head up, and features that could've been carved perfectly from stone.

But something in his movements was different, unnatural. There was a stillness to his body, a chest that didn't rise and fall with breath. A gleam in his gaze that sent a shiver down his spine.

His eyes glowed through the darkness with a light of their own, hungry and dark.

Aurora's heart stopped the moment she realized who she was looking at.

One eye bright green, like a mossy forest on a sunny spring day, and the other a deep midnight, darker than the coldest winter night.

"Nyx," she breathed.

Seven

Aurora

Aurora fell to her knees. The God of Fear and Dreams was standing before her. In *her* dream realm. She couldn't slow the emotions coursing through her veins—fear, shock, awe —there were too many for her to make sense of.

This was the only god to answer her prayers, the only one she felt like she could truly believe in.

Nyx slowly walked toward her, his feet silent as he approached. Her hair hung in front of her like a curtain, cutting off her view. But she could *feel* him. His magic. It thrummed through her like a cresting wave crashing into her over and over again.

"Stand," he commanded softly.

Her body trembled as she pushed up and stood. She was afraid to look into his eyes—was there an unspoken rule of avoiding direct eye contact with a god? Would it be rude not to? She didn't know what to do, what to say.

Aurora swallowed her fear, her gaze lifting to meet his.

He waited patiently, his hands tucked behind his back.

"You're here," she finally choked out.

He nodded slowly, his lips twitching at the corners.

Obviously he was here, but those were the only words she could manage to form in her mind, let alone speak.

His gaze followed her closely as he repositioned his hands to hang loosely at his sides. Aurora had read about the split-eyed god, but she never imagined him to be so...*beautiful.* Terrifyingly beautiful. The kind of beauty a siren possessed and used to lure someone in and snatch up their soul.

"Why are you so set on being cast out of your village?" He hummed. "You have a loving family. Friends. And prayer can be done within the confines of your mind as you lay in bed. Why risk it?"

His voice wasn't harsh—it was curious. As if she were a riddle he couldn't solve.

She considered his question, her chest aching as the truth bubbled to the surface. There was something in his gaze, something so piercing that she felt the lie die on her tongue before it even fully touched it.

Aurora had lost so much hope when her parents died. She had all but given up on *all* of the gods after that. How could the Divine be good if they allowed something so horrible to happen to her family?

Her mother and father were good people—the *best* parents, and overly gracious members of their village. They helped those with less than and gave more than they could spare. And yet, the Divine hadn't saved them. When the beast came and the darkness called, each and every god failed to keep them safe.

She was certain her parents were wrong all those years, that the Divine truly had abandoned them—that *Nyx* had abandoned the Nocturna fae.

But then Aurora was attacked in the forest, and everything changed.

Every night she spent praying with her mother, paying tribute to Nyx, came rushing back. Every promise her father whispered about the god that gifted them their magic resurfaced. Every kiss good-night they pressed against her forehead as they murmured, *"If we have the stars, then we will never be alone."*

It was clear that night she saw his eyes in her dream that he hadn't abandoned her. He never had. It was *she* who lost faith in him. She made a vow that night that she would never do that again—that she would carry on the generations of her family that prayed to Nyx.

"Because my mother taught me to always keep my word," she whispered. She held his eyes, her knees wobbling beneath his gaze. She could practically feel his magic thrumming in the surrounding air, a static that electrified the space between them. It was unlike anything she had ever felt. "No matter how hard life gets or how many riches you make for yourself, you are nothing without your word or your faith."

She swallowed, her heart hammering in her chest.

"*That* is why I risk coming out here," Aurora added breathlessly.

Nyx tilted his head to the side. "Have you not considered that you're putting yourself—the family you've been gifted—in jeopardy to carve into a silly tree?"

Aurora held his gaze. She knew what he was trying to do—of course she had considered this before. Max and Leila were *everything* to her.

"If you wish for me to stop, I will." The words flowed out of her. Though heat bloomed in her cheeks, she kept her chin lifted.

This gained a small grin from Nyx, the left corner of his mouth curling up.

"I doubt that," he replied with amusement dancing in his voice. "Regardless, I wish for you to do as you please."

"And if I wish to stop praying to you?" she dared to ask.

The right corner of his mouth kicked up, joining his left in an almost smile. "If it pleases you."

She narrowed her eyes, her awe of being in his presence fading into frustration at the way he spoke in circles.

"It pleases me, then," she huffed.

He tipped his head toward her and said, "Good. That's settled."

Her nostrils flared. She hardly ever lost her temper, her control over her emotions sealed tightly—something she had learned to do as the eldest sibling. Even as she parented her youngest siblings, her patience constantly challenged during their lessons, she never lost it like this.

Nyx turned away, his back almost to her, when she called out to him. "Why did you save me?"

He paused and glanced over his shoulder, his eyes guarded.

Aurora took a step toward him, then another, her courage growing. "That day in the woods last winter," she said slowly. "When the ignavis had me cornered. Shadows came out of thin air—certainly stronger than any I've seen—and gave me enough time to get away."

She could still hear the beast's screams in the distance as she fled to her village.

"I did not save you," he finally said. "A passing traveler, a stray ward, it could've been anything."

Her certainty wavered at the ease with which he said it.

It could've been anything.

She knew that—had told herself before she fell asleep that night that perhaps she had just gotten lucky. She had even felt a well of guilt, that maybe there *was* a passing traveler who had stopped to help and ended up being the victim.

But the *dream*...his eyes.

She wasn't insane—nor did she imagine it.

Aurora shook her head and took another step toward him, only an arm's length separating them. The wind carried his scent toward her, wrapping around her mind and senses, causing her to pause. He smelled of ice and freshly ground pepper.

"And I suppose seeing your eyes in my dream was my own mind too?" she challenged.

She could remember it as if it had been last night instead of last winter. It was too dark to see anything else, the image too fuzzy to make out. But she would never forget those eyes, and looking into them now solidified that he *was* in her dreams that night.

His gaze widened the smallest amount, a flicker of surprise shining through. "The mind is a curious thing," he murmured. His hands curled into fists and then relaxed, his posture straightening. "Still, the matters of creatures within this realm are not a concern to the gods. Especially not within the context of a single life. We see so much more than you can imagine."

While that may have been true, she wasn't entirely convinced. Call it stupidity or naivety, she still didn't believe him.

Aurora gathered what remained of her courage and said, "Then why are you here?"

Moonlight shone through the trees, casting light across the snowy ground. Nyx's feathered coat gleamed like a blanket of night wrapped around him—though she doubted gods were affected by things as simple as the cold.

Nyx looked up, his gaze following a shooting star as it streamed through the sky. "I would prefer for you to live, Aurora."

Her mouth tilted into a frown. She may have been fae, but all fae died eventually. Immortal didn't mean indestructible. Still, his words didn't make any sense.

"You don't care about any of us, but you want *me* to live?" she questioned. "Do all gods contradict themselves, or just you?"

The second question slipped out before she could stop it. Ice spread through her chest as the words hung in the air. It was too far, and she knew it, yet she couldn't stop herself. She wanted to know more about him—about all the gods.

How could she *not* ask?

Nyx paused, his gaze lingering on the sky. "Things you cannot imagine reside in the wood." He huffed a laugh, the sound deep and throaty. "Be more careful."

Be *more?* All she ever did was *be careful.*

They all had to—the entire village; their lives depended on it. They had been hunted down beneath the veil of midnight for years by a creature they couldn't catch. They were as defenseless as humans, their magic unable to stop whatever it was that terrorized them.

If Aurora knew anything, it was *careful*.

His warning felt empty, as if he didn't realize just how much the village had endured while trying to stay safe. Though, she supposed, why *would* he care? How would he know? As far as she knew, there weren't any others that prayed to him—no others that asked for his help or guidance.

But here she was, in front of someone who might be capable of helping.

Even if she could get a small clue that could help keep her siblings safe, she had to try.

"Do you know what's taking and killing the villagers?" She couldn't stop the question from flowing out of her mouth.

He tilted his head to the side and simply said, "I do."

She waited for him to say more, but that was all the answer he seemed inclined to give.

This time, she didn't stop him as he turned away.

His feet lifted, and her mouth fell open as he floated from the ground, his cape of feathers billowing behind him as if he had wings of his own. Aurora was left standing in the forest of her dreams with nothing but wisps of shadows in his wake.

Eight

Nyx

He saw her tonight. Not in the way he usually did from afar or through the eyes of his raven.

This time, he stood before her in his own flesh.

So different from gazing at her while she prayed over the past year. Her plea for help last winter had been full of such clear and raw emotions that it struck a chord deep within him. A chord that had been asleep for hundreds of years.

His heart—a frozen and rotted thing that lay still within his chest—had felt...something. A flicker. A twinge. It didn't beat, not entirely. But it wasn't as cold. There was now a soft warmth that danced around the edges of his damned soul.

How could he turn away from a voice that managed to do that?

While his sisters and brothers couldn't be bothered with one cry for help out of thousands, he heard her. And he had been hearing her ever since. Every prayer, every inch she carved into bark beneath the moon, he was there. Watching. Waiting.

Nyx never knew *what* exactly he was waiting on. For her to tire of having to hide from the world? She had to realize eventually that placing her faith in him was futile. Still, that day hadn't come. Each time, he simply watched from above, perched on the highest limb with his feet dangling beneath him.

He was invisible to her, watching as she carved his symbol into trees and murmured prayers, unknowing that he was hovering nearby. His curse had left him invisible to the realm, nothing more than a vapor in the wind or a whisper in the breeze.

This fae—who didn't possess any extraordinary magic—had been the first to see him in *decades*. Nyx had been drifting through the realm, floating in front of humans and fae alike, with them none the wiser. He watched as they slept and as they awoke. Their lives became more boring the longer he was forced to be nothing more than a ghost; his life consisted of being an outsider looking in.

The longer his curse held him in this prison, the more he retreated to his home, opting to ignore that the mortals existed at all.

There was a time when he was freely given the remedy for his curse, when he was worshipped by many and loved by the masses. He hated to rely on the mortals, to need them in order to be whole.

Though perhaps that's why it was a curse.

The thing he loathed was the very thing that kept him most powerful.

When they decided he wasn't one of the Divine worth praying to, he was all too eager to blame them. Ignore any stray half-hearted cries for help that were flung his way.

But then there was the panicked prayer shouted out to him on a frigid winter night. Years ago, it may have been one voice of many that prayed to him, but things had changed. That night, it was like a bell chiming in the dead of night. He heard it loud and clear, enough so that his curiosity got the better of him.

He followed the thread that attached the prayer to the soul saying it, all the way to a snowy forest outside the small town of Morior. What he found made him understand why this fae had called out to him: a woman being attacked by a creature of the dark—one that had wandered a little too far from its normal habitat.

The creature had noticed his presence immediately, pausing to look in his general direction. Nyx still didn't know why he took interest in helping this girl, but he helped her all the same. He had given her enough time to get away before using his shadows to rip the bird apart piece by piece. To pluck the creature feather by feather.

What he wasn't expecting was to visit her in her dreams.

Nyx waited until she fell asleep, curious what a mind like hers would hold. But the moment he snuck into her head—her dreams—her eyes had widened as if she had seen a ghost. As if she could see *him*.

He got out of there as quickly as he had entered, but it was enough to make him want to know more about why this ordinary woman from a small town next to the Zenovia Mountains could see him when no one else could.

It was just enough to make him want to know her.

There was always a curiosity he had when he watched her, an obsession that started as saving a woman in the woods and turned into something deeper. He was never meant to reveal himself to her.

He never thought he *could* reveal himself, even if he wanted to, not with the way his magic had dimmed the last few decades. But somehow, he had done just that.

Aurora saw him in her dreams the night she was attacked. An unfortunate development that surprised him—and not much surprised him anymore.

His curse had left him invisible to the realm. To all except Aurora...

Nyx shook his head, reorienting himself to his crumbling home.

Now that he had met her once, perhaps this curiosity would fade. Perhaps it had merely been a small itch he needed to scratch to get over it.

It would only serve to harm her tand her village if he continued to go back. They were already a playground for Vidaris, being so close to her domain—they didn't need him adding to the death toll.

There were more pressing matters he needed to focus on. Things with Vidaris had escalated this past century, the goddess growing hungrier for blood and chaos. War was on the horizon, possibly in a few years' time.

The girl was a distraction, nothing more.

Nine

Aurora

Aurora floated through her day, attempting to combine what she imagined Nyx to be and the Nyx she met last night. He was a *god*—seemingly flesh and blood, not just one she heard about in stories or read in texts.

She had never met anyone who had seen—let alone spoken to—one of the gods. Even the stories of those who had seen Nyx were always told by a friend of a friend.

He refused to admit he saved her last winter, though she was certain he had. He also said that gods didn't care about creatures of the realm, yet he came to warn Aurora to be more careful.

It was an odd thing to meet the god she prayed to. In a way, it made him seem less indestructible. As if seeing him look like *almost* any other fae made her forget what he was capable of. Forget who he was.

But he was still the god that saved her, and she wouldn't forget it. That was what mattered the most.

He may have seemed ordinary, but his power radiated off of him. It was the small fissure in his "ordinary" presence that reminded her who he was. There was a stiffness to his movements—an unnatural grace his body possessed.

Aurora vowed her devotion to him for what he had done, and she wouldn't take it back now.

***

The next day, she thought of his split irises and how they opposed each other. And the day after, she wondered why he decided to appear in *her* dreams.

Beyond that, there was a singular thought that gnawed at her. What she couldn't get out of her mind was that he knew what was terrorizing her village. Of course he did—he was a god. Knowing for certain that he knew what was causing it brought a flurry of questions to her thoughts.

The days bled into weeks, wondering when he would show back up so she could ask him about the monster terrorizing the village. She wasn't foolish enough to believe he would simply tell her, but if she could get even a small *glimpse* of the truth, maybe it could help keep her and her family safe.

She didn't pause her visits to the wood after meeting him. In fact, she had found herself going consistently every three midnights since. She had shifted from offering prayers of thanksgiving to asking a million questions.

Why didn't he stop the creature? Where did the creature come from? Was it only terrorizing her village because they were so isolated?

Aurora felt Maliena's lingering stares each time they crossed paths near curfew. Her friend never stopped her—only posed a question or two. She never forced her to quit.

Her curiosity in seeing him again, mixed with the need to find out what plagued her village, kept her going. Villagers were still going missing, and if Nyx knew, she was going to find out how to stop it.

***

She lay in her bed that night, her mind running rampant. It had been a full moon phase since she had seen Nyx in the wood, but her hope of finding out more hadn't lessened. She gripped the wooden carved star while she slipped into her dreams.

This time, she found herself in the middle of Lac Noir, the night sky burning above her. In her dreams, there was no cold, only a constant cool breeze, as if it were a sunny autumn day. Just the way she liked it.

Her limbs felt twice their weight as she walked on the ice, her heart thumping in rhythm to her steps.

Then, a wave of energy slammed into her. It wrapped around her body, caressing her skin like tendrils of darkness. It snaked up and down her spine, leaving chills in its wake. She knew that feeling—had felt it twice before.

"You didn't come to the wood today," a voice rumbled from behind her.

She spun around, unable to stop the gasp that came from her lips.

All the questions she'd been dying to ask Nyx vanished the moment her eyes met his. Her frantic thoughts quieted, her heart pounding against her chest as he watched her. The memory of his gaze didn't compare to the way it glowed in the moonlight now.

Nyx was in her dreams...*again.*

He raised a brow, and she realized he was waiting on a response.

With a palm pressed to her chest, she said, "Max wasn't sleeping well, so I couldn't leave without him noticing."

Nyx hummed and folded his hands behind his back. "I see."

An awkward silence stretched between them, one Aurora wanted to fill the moment it started. She had never done well with silence.

"Why are you here?" she asked tentatively, her stomach turning at the possibilities of his answer—if he would answer at all.

Looking at him now, at the curious glint in his eyes, he looked ordinary, just as he did the night they had met. But he *was* a god, his movements unnaturally still—cold and stiff.

"As I said..." He hesitated, then continued, his voice a low hum, "You weren't in the forest as you usually are on this day."

She had found a routine in praying to him, but she hardly thought missing one evening would warrant his concern... Or whatever this was. If she had known breaking her pattern would've gotten a visit from him, she would've done it far sooner.

But never would she have guessed he would *notice* her absence.

The realization that perhaps he had been paying attention to her as much as she had him knocked the breath from her lungs.

Breathless, she grappled with what to say. The only thing that had been on her mind was the hope of enlisting his help with the creature plaguing her village, but now she found a new flurry of thoughts invading her mind.

"And a visit to me was required to find out why?" Confusion swirled inside of her, followed by an overwhelming need to know *more*. She had important questions for him, and these weren't among them. But they tumbled out regardless. "If you wanted to know, couldn't you just...watch what I'm doing?"

It seemed absurd to suggest he would *want* to watch her. But for him to be anything less than knowledgeable about all things in this world was even further out of the realm of possibilities.

Nyx watched her closely, his eyes tracking every muscle she moved. "It doesn't work that way for the lesser gods."

Her brows jumped up. She hadn't expected him to answer so plainly—he seemed to favor talking around something rather than answering directly. She tucked away that information and remained quiet, silently urging him to continue.

He leaned his back against a tree sprouting up out of the icy lake and tilted his face up to the sky. She mirrored his movements and peered up to watch the stars.

Just when she thought he wouldn't say anything more, he said, "Eurydice sees all—Vidaris would too if she weren't confined to the Vale." His odd smile faded, his tone easing into how it sounded when they met. Disinterested. "Only when you pray to me can I see you."

She couldn't hide the surprise on her face as a shudder rippled through her. Her fingers trembled as she asked, "So when I didn't pray this evening..."

"I couldn't see you," he finished. "And you should know that the carving under your floorboard could get you caught."

Aurora froze.

The possibility wasn't lost on her, but the carving was all she had left of her parents. There had been a number of times she considered tossing it out or burning it for the sake of her siblings, but each time she went to destroy it, her mother's voice would surface in her mind, and she couldn't bear to part with it.

She drew in a tight breath and turned to look at him, his face still tilted toward the sky. Warmth spread through her chest as she realized the intimacy in his question.

Perhaps he had been watching her far longer than she thought.

Breathless, she whispered, "How do you know about that?"

Without looking at her, he laughed—a soft sound that she wouldn't have heard if she weren't standing so close.

"You hold it sometimes when you pray to me." He shook his head. "If someone found the depth you've gone to hide it, I fear it wouldn't sit well. It may not be enough to accuse you, but it would be enough to raise suspicions."

Aurora blinked. His voice was formal, as if reciting recipe ingredients. But as he turned to look at her, waiting for her response, she saw something more. His eyes were conflicted, his brows drawn slightly together.

"I'll be careful," she promised.

She couldn't read him, couldn't figure out what thoughts were running through his mind. Unlike him, she imagined she wore her emotions on her sleeve, the book opened to a page she didn't want anyone to read—as if she had no say in keeping it hidden.

"I have questions," she said slowly. "A lot."

He nodded, as if expecting her words. "A truth for an answer, then."

She thought on it, his offer making her pause.

Gods loved to bargain. It was something she had always read in texts and heard in stories—no matter how they differed otherwise, they always had the same message: never bargain with a god.

The gods were sneakier than the eldest of fae, more cunning than a trained Aegis with centuries of experience. She overheard a story when she was little—had snuck out of bed to get a snack and found her parents whispering. As much as her parents respected all of the Divine, they knew not to trust their deals. Her mother had said, *"To bargain with a god is to bargain with death."*

A "no" sat on the tip of her tongue. She opened her mouth, and Nyx smiled, as if he expected this too.

But what if she said yes? What if that one word could change the course of her life? It was the not knowing—the endless possibilities— that lay ahead that had her answering against every instinct in her body.

She *meant* to say no, but what came out was "Yes, okay."

He saved her last winter, after all, and a truth in exchange for answers from him seemed like a fair trade.

"But you have to answer a question before you ask me a truth," she added. "And if you don't answer the question directly, then I don't have to answer the truth directly."

She thought through anything else he could do to manipulate the bargain, but hoped those two rules would cover the bases well enough.

"Agreed." He held out a hand.

Her gaze dropped to where it hovered in front of her. Slowly, she reached up and clasped her hand in his. If she thought being *near* the weight of his power was intense, then she was sorely mistaken. As her skin met his, her knees threatened to buckle. Her stomach flipped upside down, and she begged her pulse to slow.

She squeezed his hand tighter. When she looked back up at him, his eyes were set on where their palms were joined, fingers grazing wrists.

"I think that's enough for tonight," he said abruptly as he released her. "Think on your first question."

His words sank in. She hadn't thought she would see him tonight, let alone more often.

"You'll be back?" she asked hesitantly.

His eyes flashed with delight. "Your first question came quickly."

Her face flushed. "That wasn't meant—"

"But a question nonetheless."

Aurora felt like a mouse caught between the claws of a cat. They had just made the agreement, and she had already made a mistake.

"I will be back," he answered with a light lilt in his voice. She wanted to ask *why*, but bit her lip to keep from saying more. "My turn."

As the words left his mouth, fear gathered in her chest. Had she truly been dense enough to make a deal with a god?

"Will you stop worshiping me in the wood like I have asked?"

"You didn't *technically* ask me to stop," she whispered.

Nyx tilted his head to the side and frowned. "But you won't stop." There was no question in his voice, the answer already clear.

Aurora shook her head. She wouldn't stop—she had never been the type to give up when things got hard. It made her want to do it all the same, if not more. It was the way she learned to pay proper tribute, the way her parents had taught her and their parents before them. Tradition was all she had left.

"Then you leave me no choice."

The world around her slammed into darkness.

Her eyes snapped open, and she found herself back in her room, no longer in her dreams.

She brushed her fingers beneath her pillow, needing to feel the shape of her carved star, only to find the space empty. Her heart raced, and she sat up, lifting her pillow and frantically pushing her blanket to the side. It wasn't there.

The carving wasn't under the bed or in the hiding place in the floorboards. Her panic set in, taking control of her lungs and squeezing. She saw her mother's face fading, her voice a whisper as she lost the final connection to her.

Nyx's voice rumbled through her mind, the sadness reflected in his eyes haunting her as she wrestled with the meaning of his words— *Then you leave me no choice.*

Ten

Aurora

Aurora shoved fresh goat cheese into her wagon—a little harder than necessary, causing the cheese to lump unevenly to one side.

"It was mine," she huffed.

Nyx hadn't just stolen what was *hers*. He had taken what was left of her parents.

To him, she may have seemed like a child who had her toy stolen, but she didn't care. Nyx didn't understand what the carving meant to her, what it had meant to her family, having been passed down from mother to daughter for generations.

He may even have been right—that it was too dangerous to have—but that was *her* decision to make, not his.

"I want it back, Nyx," she grumbled out loud. More of a statement than a prayer meant for him. But she wouldn't be upset if he *happened* to hear it. "Or I'll just carve another."

There wasn't much in this realm that belonged to her. She shared her room with Max, her clothes with Leila, and her trade with both of them. That tiny carving was hers and only hers.

Her family's cottage was warm and cozy, the hearth stoked to a steady flame. Aurora's eyes drifted to where the reddened flames were crackling in the brick-framed cutout. Unease worked its way into her chest, settling against it like a boulder. The fire would one day come for her. It was the only thing she was certain of.

"She just wandered away!" A shrill voice from outside pierced the stillness of the cottage, muffled by the wooden slats in front of her. "She's young, she likes to explore—"

The voice was cut off.

Aurora's spine snapped straight when the screaming began. She pushed to her feet, leaving her wagon behind as she ran toward the sound.

Max and Leila were out doing chores—Max helped Maliena with a few things while Leila gathered wood. She *knew* that voice; it was one of Leila's friends, a girl a few years older than her.

She stumbled down the worn path along Lac Noir, her feet numb as her thin leather flats sank into the snow. She hadn't bothered putting her winter boots on; the scream carried her in a haze to the village's center.

Please don't be Leila, please don't be Leila, she chanted in her mind, sending every prayer she could to Nyx.

The monster had never taken someone during the day, but that didn't mean it wouldn't.

Blood rushed in her ears, filling her head until she felt almost too dizzy to stand. But her feet continued to move, despite her heart threatening to give out along the way. It felt as if her head was stuck beneath the murky lake water, the sounds around her muted, her vision blurry.

It wasn't until she reached the gathered crowd and saw a familiar brown five-strand braid that her senses snapped back into place. Everything was too loud, too much at once. The screaming was still going, and people had started crying.

Aurora couldn't see what everyone had gathered around, but she didn't care. She raced for her sister, her clothes feeling too scratchy and her hair feeling too heavy on her head.

She threw her arms around Leila, her sister emitting a small *umph* at the forceful contact.

Leila looked over her shoulder, her eyes glistening. "I'm okay," she whispered as she spun toward her, sensing Aurora's panic.

Aurora tightened her arms around Leila's shoulders. They had already lost their parents; she and Max couldn't handle losing Leila, too. And at this moment, Leila looked so much younger—so much like the day they had lost their parents.

Guilt gnawed at the edges of Aurora's heart. She was playing with fire when it came to Nyx. Leila and Max had grown so much and were so much more capable of taking care of themselves now. But they still needed each other—even if some days it felt like Aurora needed them more than they needed her.

"It was Nora," Leila added, drawing Aurora's attention back to her. "She went missing last night, and Leah thought she could find her, but..."

She didn't have to finish saying it. *Only her bones were left.*

It should've been normal to find villagers missing by now, but it didn't get easier with each life lost. Each time someone was taken, it made the fear sink deeper into everyone's thoughts.

"Someone else must be calling this darkness on us," a woman hissed from Aurora's left. "This creature is the dark gods' doing."

A man behind her grunted his agreement and said, "Or it *is* one of the dark gods." Aurora held her breath, knowing where this was going. "Nyx is feeding off our fear to garner more power. He doesn't have anyone sacrificing or praying to him anymore, so he's resorted to other means."

Mumbles of agreement simmered through the crowd. Curses were flung at Nyx as they blamed him for the missing girl.

"We need to send someone to the palace to enlist more help," someone jumped in. "Maybe we can make a plea at the Celestial Temple for the Sacred to pray to Eurydice on our behalf."

The whispers quieted.

Aurora knew it would be useless. Whatever was plaguing their village wasn't a concern of Eurydice—why else would it still be hunting them down? The people here had been praying for years to be rid of this faceless creature, and yet another had been taken.

As much as Aurora knew she should consider the possibility of it being Nyx, she didn't.

She knew how foolish it was—this blind faith that led her to believe he wasn't the one doing it. He wouldn't need to hide beneath the guise of stealing stray villagers after dark. Nyx was a *god*. If he wanted to, he could snatch them from their beds.

The thing doing this behaved like a scared animal. It picked off people one by one, and never in crowded areas like the village itself. Always in the wood, always at night.

And Nyx was anything but scared.

Aurora steered her sister back to their cottage, only making a brief stop to pick up Max and fill Maliena in on what had happened to Nora. The cleaned bones of the girl had been left on the edge of the village, just as they always were. A trophy the creature left to be found, leaving the village to guess who it was, only figuring it out once their bed was empty and they hadn't been seen since the day before.

With a grim set to her jaw, Maliena offered to stay with Leila and Max while Aurora went to the trading post to find grain for supper. Aurora tried to refuse, but if she were being honest, it eased an enormous weight off her shoulders knowing her siblings would be looked after while she was gone.

Even if the creature had only ever struck beneath the midnight moon, it still pained her to leave them alone for too long.

Worry nipped at Aurora's chest as she stomped across the frozen lake to the trading post, wagon in tow. She huffed, her breath coming out in tiny clouds.

The morning was clear, the sun far too bright for the gloom hanging over her village. She had just reached the middle of the frozen lake—the path well-known though unmarked—when the fog billowed in.

The thick vapor settled around the lake, making it impossible to see either bank. It wasn't the first time the cloudy haze had gathered here; in fact, she found it clinging around the ice more often than not.

But something about this was different—so hazy that she could hardly see her wagon behind her or her feet beneath her.

Ice slithered along Aurora's spine, and she froze, fingers tightening around the wooden handle.

A lone bird cried above her, so close to her that she could hear the beating of its wings as it skated over her head. Even with the fog obstructing her view of the bird, she knew it was her raven.

The handle became unbearably cold, the wood freezing her fingers into a painful grip. It was the kind of deep cold that could have been fire or ice.

She yelped and let go. It clattered to the ground—or at least she assumed it did since the lake was covered in a soft powder from last night's snowfall.

She crouched down, blindly feeling for the handle. Her fingers met only snow and ice, even though the handle should have been *right* there. She crawled forward, reaching for the wagon itself, but it too had vanished.

The white haze surrounded her like she had been swallowed up by the fog and was stuck in its belly. Her need to find the wagon dissipated as she realized she couldn't see how to get off the lake. And she *needed* to see to ensure she wasn't stepping on a weak spot in the ice.

If she were to fall through, no one would be fast enough to save her—let alone see her in this weather. Panic gripped her throat and constricted her breathing.

The world around her was nothing—devoid of color. She briefly wondered if she had lost her sight. She had never been in a fog like this before.

She scrambled to her feet, hoping she could feel around for a tree she recognized and get back on the path. The wagon could wait, but she couldn't stay stranded in the middle of the lake.

With her hands stretched out in front of her, she slowly took a step forward. She could only see down to her elbow, the rest of her arms veiled beneath the blanket of fog. She kept going, waiting for her hand to meet bark...*or* the gnashing teeth of a monster. The skin on her palms prickled, hoping it would be the former.

But her hands met neither as she wandered through the fog. Her heart hammered in her chest the longer she went without finding a tree. No matter where she was on the lake, the odds of *not* coming across a tree yet were incredibly slim. She should've found one by now, should've even reached the edge.

Unless she was going in circles without realizing it.

Her hands began to shake, and she was certain she was going to be the unnamed monster's next victim.

A thought tugged at her mind to pray to Nyx. Her heart sped faster than she thought possible, the beat rapidly pounding against her chest in a painful rhythm. She could ask him for guidance, could ask for clarity or—

Her raven cawed again. In its wake, a path cleared through the fog. She could see straight through it like a tunnel leading to the forest.

The bank was unfamiliar to her, surrounded by odd trees.

She was desperate to get off the ice, so when she saw her raven disappear into the depths of the strange wood, she didn't hesitate to follow it.

Eleven

Aurora

The forest wasn't one that Aurora recognized. She had grown up with these trees. Some that had been saplings when she was a child now towered over her. Even without her trek to and from the trading post, she knew this area like the back of her hand.

But this wasn't her forest, and these weren't her trees.

She glanced over her shoulder, seeing a white haze still covering the lake. Her options were to stumble through it or find another way back home. Since this was the only path she could *see*, it seemed this was the only one worth exploring—better than wandering aimlessly through an unmarked forest.

So, she shuffled ahead quicker, hoping that since her raven was flying over her, it meant she was safe.

"Where are we going?" Aurora asked the midnight-feathered bird above.

As suspected, it didn't answer. It continued its flight a few branches overhead and guided her through the forest.

She hoped more than anything that the forest wasn't playing

tricks on her. The Cimmerian Forest was known to be a place where you could not always believe what your eyes were seeing and what your ears were hearing. Though that was mainly a warning given to outsiders, those who hadn't grown up here. The trees didn't recognize them, didn't trust them. So, it played tricks to keep them out, sending them back to where they came from.

Aurora never worried about their illusions as a child when she explored; she drank the water from the river that seeped into their roots, ate the fruit that ripened on their branches.

The forest knew her.

But she doubted she wasn't to be their latest victim the further she walked into the woods.

After a few steps, the sun began to set, and the winter insects chirped their evening song. Aurora froze, watching in horror as the light above her dimmed into darkness within the span of a few breaths.

It shouldn't have been close to midday yet—let alone night.

She quickened her pace, running to the beat of her racing heart. The trees were most definitely playing a trick on her.

Her raven disappeared into the branches ahead, and terror gripped her by the throat.

"Wait!" she screamed.

Branches stretched toward her as she ran, reaching out to graze her arms and legs.

She had to get out of the forest.

As much as she wanted to turn around and try the lake again, she had gone too far now. With the sun gone and the sky dark, she would have no chance of making it back alone.

She sped toward the direction she last saw the raven, hoping this was all a nightmare.

An image flashed through her mind: her bones being found. Her siblings realizing her bed was empty. Their tears as they cried out for her. Maliena trying to help them survive on their own.

She kept going, kept pushing, her siblings' faces in the forefront of her thoughts as she pressed ahead.

The moment she made it to where the raven had been, she saw an opening in the trees. She slammed to a halt and leaned over to grasp her knees. Her breath was coming in quick gasps, and she tried to force her breathing to slow.

Once she had calmed down enough, she looked around the small clearing to get her bearings. But the moment her eyes lifted to the sky, her skin began to prickle with a bone-seeping cold.

Ice licked up her spine just as it had in the fog.

This sky wasn't her sky. The stars were all wrong; the constellations that had been there for millennia were gone. She didn't recognize the stars above, nor the trees below.

Her hands shook, and she wished she had stayed on the lake.

The piercing cry of a bird screeched from her right, and she whirled toward it. She found her raven sitting atop a stone staircase.

Her eyes widened as she took in the building before her, which hadn't been there a moment ago. The cracked staircase, half-covered in moss, led to a grand temple—or what was left of one. Ivy hung over the entrance, a crooked cutout in the stone that looked like it had once been adorned with beautiful etchings but was now plagued with cracks.

The whole temple was half-crumbling from what she could see of it. The stairs went up so high, they looked as if they were trying to reach the glorious afterlife of Caelum.

She took a small step forward, but warning bells sounded in her mind, urging her to stop. When she hesitated, her raven took flight off the stone step and landed on her shoulder.

A feeling of calm washed over her as it perched there, and she walked until her winter boots found the bottom of the staircase. Her curiosity tugged her up, over the mossy patches sprawling across the stone, all the way to the crooked entrance.

With a final glance at the odd stars, she stepped over the threshold.

Her pulse raced, and she hesitated. The raven fluttered its wings and scooted closer to her neck.

She had already pushed ahead this far. What other choice did she have but to keep going?

After taking a deep breath, she continued ahead, walking through a damp and dark hallway that could've been classified as a tunnel. She had to hunch down, the ceiling low and the rounded sides close together. The distant sound of water dripping echoed around her as she made her way along to where the glow of the moon gleamed, illuminating the tunnel's end.

She realized why the moonlight was streaming in once she stepped into the open room. The roof had partially collapsed, leaving space for light to brighten what would've been a pitch-black room. At least she could see what she was getting herself into.

Aurora's raven fluttered its wings and hopped off her shoulder. It hovered in front of her, its eyes piercing, before turning to guide her through the broken and moss-covered temple.

It had led her this far, so why stop now?

A small stone bench rested beneath partially shattered stained-glass windows. Ivy crawled over the bench, encasing it in vegetation. Aurora followed the bird toward it, and her gaze caught on the tiny wooden object resting on the seat. It sat atop a thick crack along the middle of the bench, one that left it with the back portion too high and the front slightly lower, uneven and broken like the rest of this place.

The wood was just as she remembered it. She picked it up and inspected it closer; a chunk she had accidentally cut too deep rested in the center, just as it should. One point was dulled on the tip from her constantly running her thumb over it.

She gasped. "My carving?"

Whatever this strange place was, it wasn't a coincidence that her star was here. It didn't end up here by chance, and neither had the raven led her to it by mistake.

Her pulse thrashed as she made sense of what this could mean. She hadn't lost her star. Nyx's ominous words about "having no other choice" played in her mind.

This was Nyx's doing.

Twelve

Aurora

Just when she thought he had taken one of her only true belongings, Nyx had brought Aurora here, where he'd left the carving for her to find. Her mind whirled with the possibilities of why. What did he have to gain? Was it truly as simple as him enjoying her company?

She shook her head, remembering how easily he could wipe an entire village—or multiple villages—off the map in seconds if he wanted to. Nyx was a god. One who had paid her more kindnesses than she might have deserved.

But the gods were dangerous beings, not bound by good or evil, and without a moral compass to guide them. They were immortal, the beginning and the end. And, most importantly, they often did what was beneficial to them. Especially the dark gods.

Aurora may have prayed to Nyx, may have believed in him far more than the others, but she wasn't oblivious to him being considered a dark god. She always thought him to be misplaced, pulled into a title he didn't deserve, all because he was the God of Fear and Dreams.

Above all that, he had saved her last winter. Even if he had yet to admit it.

She clutched the little wooden star to her chest.

Follow the raven home.

She gasped as the words drifted in the air around her.

A familiar slither of ice ran down her spine, causing her shoulders to shiver at the caress. She knew that feeling—had felt it the night Nyx saved her and again when the raven led her through the fog. It felt like a power so ancient and primal that every fiber in her body reacted to it.

Her magic answered in tandem, reaching out to grasp onto the source of the power. Nyx.

She felt the power recede, along with the ice grazing her spine.

"Wait!" she shouted into the moonlit temple, her breathless voice bouncing off the damp stone walls. "Please, Nyx."

The receding paused, like one foot was in while the other was already out.

"Why am I here?"

Wherever here *is*, she thought.

The temple remained silent. Her raven perched on the bench in front of her and turned its head to the side, watching her.

Follow the raven home.

The words settled into the air around her, grave and quiet. It didn't sound like Nyx, but she could feel it. Feel *him*.

"Why did you bring me here?" she tried again, and this time her voice was stronger—more confident. Her feet stayed planted in the same spot.

It may not have been wise to push a god like this, but something inside her couldn't help it. He had brought her this far, and she wanted to know why.

She crossed her arms, waiting for a response.

The raven flew away, flitting through a shattered windowpane.

Still, she refused to move.

A heavy sigh filled the space behind her. "Do you ever just do what you're told?"

She briefly mused that it actually seemed like it was only with him that she *didn't* do what she was told.

Before turning toward him, she unfolded her arms and smiled down at her wooden star. Slowly, she twisted to face where his voice had come from.

Her mouth parted as her gaze met his. She had almost thought she was used to seeing him—that she would remain the picture of calm and collected when she turned. But there was no getting used to his presence.

He floated slightly off the ground, his cape of feathers rustling against a frosty breeze. She watched as he lowered to the ground. His split-colored irises were impossible to look away from.

Even standing ten paces away—feet now firmly settled on the damp stone—he towered over her, his frame imposing.

But it still made little sense why he was here, where she was. It was as if he couldn't stay away.

She pressed her lips together, confusion tugging at her chest.

Then she remembered their deal—a question for a truth.

"Where are we right now?" she asked.

He started to shake his head, but she cut him off before he could reject her question.

"A question for a truth," she reminded him, hoping he would play along.

The corners of his mouth curved up as his eyes flashed with what she could only guess was delight, and he nodded. "I want to show you something," he said gently. Her brows pressed together, not seeing how this answered what she had asked. "It will make sense once we get there."

She blinked, certain she hadn't heard him right. "My wagon—"

"Will be waiting for you where you left it," he assured her. "With double what you intended to trade for."

She swallowed, the curiosity beginning to outweigh her hesitation. "And if I don't want to go with you?"

A part of her wanted to see what he would do when pushed—as bad an idea as that likely was.

"Then I will respect it." His response was so matter-of-fact, it was as if there was no alternative. He took a step closer, and she took one away, the backs of her knees hitting the icy bench behind her. But then he froze and tilted his head to the side. "Are you afraid of me, Aurora?"

As much as she wanted to say yes—felt like she *should* be saying yes—she knew she couldn't lie to him. She wasn't afraid of him...and that frightened her more than anything.

"No," she breathed.

His eyes gleamed with delight once more. "Then would you like to return home or come with me?" he continued.

Something inside her awoke with his question, along with a warmth that gathered deep in her stomach. She tucked her star into her pocket and said, "With you."

He held out a hand. "Follow me."

Thirteen

Aurora

She slipped her hand into his, their palms melding together—Nyx's icy and hard, while Aurora's were soft and warm. It took all of her concentration not to stare down at where they were joined together.

"Where are we going?" she asked.

He guided them through the temple, navigating from the open room into a hallway—this one normal-sized with high ceilings and a wide path to walk through—to a series of rooms with no doors.

Instead of answering, he simply glanced at her. His eyes blazed into her, causing heat to lick up her spine. There was something dark in his gaze, the kind of darkness in which she could get lost and never be found.

The glance caused her heart to speed up. She briefly wondered if gods could hear the patter of a fae's heart—or, worse, if they could sense their emotion.

They passed small rooms, mostly bare save for a few pieces of partially broken furniture. She wanted to ask what they were, but she decided she didn't want to owe him any more truths.

He stopped in front of the last entryway in the hall, the inside too dark to see what awaited them. When he pulled her in behind him, she was plunged into darkness.

Aurora's breath came out faster, her lungs frozen as they stood in the dark. If Nyx noticed, he made no sign of it.

A tiny glowing orb twinkled to life above them, so small it didn't provide any lighting in the room. But then another orb glittered awake, followed by ten, then fifty more, until the entire ceiling—so high it could've been the start of Caelum—was a constellation of stars.

There was enough light to see what was in front of them. Statues rested in the center of the room, positioned atop a circular rock structure. Each statue stood on its own pillar; the pillars were connected by small ledges to form the circle.

Seven statues. One for each god. They were all facing the center, which appeared empty and open—they seemed to look down at something.

Aurora stepped closer, dropping Nyx's hand as she approached the center of the statues.

A crystal star was carved into the stone floor, a soft glow emanating from it. It pulsed, almost like a heartbeat. She crouched down and reached for it, a string in her chest yanking her closer. The moment her fingers hovered above it, a white flame roared to life, encircling it.

Aurora gasped as the flame grazed her skin. She tried to get away from it, only she couldn't move—couldn't jump back. Something was holding her in place, her hand locked within the white fire.

The vision of her dying within flames slammed into her mind. Warning bells went off in her head, and panic gripped her chest. Her nightmare was finally coming to fruition.

"Breathe, Aurora." Nyx's voice was right beside her, speaking so quietly that he had to be inches away from her ear. She wanted to look, but her eyes couldn't seem to move from the fire. "I won't hurt you."

She knew that, but this was a blazing fire in a temple she had never been to and—

It wasn't hot. It was freezing.

His words sank in. *I* won't hurt you.

The flame was his—his magic.

Without another thought, the invisible chains holding her in place vanished. She fell to her knees and pulled her hand away, cradling it to her chest though the skin was unburned.

Cold arms wrapped slowly around her, stiff and awkward.

Once her breathing had evened, she expected him to move away. But they stayed like that—her on her knees as he held her like it was the first time he had ever done this with someone.

The panic dissipated, and she could feel every place his body touched hers. The terror changed into something else. Something hot that slithered down her spine and around to her stomach, settling low in her abdomen.

Nyx was holding her...and she found she liked it.

"Each god has their own temple—a place we find solace in that no other god can step foot into," he began quietly.

She kept her eyes on the white flame and, for the first time, realized she wasn't afraid of being near a fire.

"So, this is your home?" She looked around the room, which was just as cracked and crumbling as the main room where she'd found the wooden star. Her cottage wasn't grand or beautiful, but it made her sad that this was where he called home.

"Of sorts."

A non-answer, but it said all he needed to say.

"And you're just here..." Her voice trailed off, and his arms tightened around her. "Alone?"

He *tsked* and let go of her. Her body warmed the moment his cool touch left hers—yet heat somehow was left in his wake, too.

"I've lost count of how many answers I've given," he responded. "Let's settle on three."

She opened her mouth, certain it was only two—but he beat her to it.

"If you could have any wish granted, what would it be?"

Nyx's question surprised her, and she turned to face him, both still on the ground. He was sitting with his legs crossed, his hands resting lightly on his knees. His midnight hair had shifted over his eyes, somehow unkempt and perfectly positioned at the same time. She couldn't look away from his gaze, from the split irises that sparkled against the firelight.

And Aurora certainly couldn't help but notice the way he watched her back, his brows pulled together and head tilted toward the side as he waited for her to answer.

She cleared her throat and thought about his question for a moment. Every wish she had dreamt of raced through her mind. There was a cracked pot that leaked water as it boiled that needed fixing. Then there were her family's plates that were always far too empty in the winter. But if she could bring her parents back somehow, she wouldn't hesitate to trade anything to make that happen.

"My parents—"

"I cannot bring back those that have passed onto Caelum," he interjected quietly. "As much as I'd like to."

Disappointment washed over her, but she wasn't surprised. So, she asked for the next best thing—the reason her parents were taken from her. The image of Max being out past curfew slammed into her, stirring a worry deep in her belly at the thought of it happening again.

But beneath that worry was something stronger. More solid. A fierce need to protect her siblings and figure out the root of her anxiety.

"The creature that plagues my village," Aurora began. Her fingers were trembling, but she held her voice even. "If I could have one thing, it would be for us to be free from it."

She held her breath, wondering if this was a part of the game or if he intended to help.

He paused, the room silent save for the crackling of the icy flames in front of them. She was dying to ask if he knew what the beast was, but she held herself back, careful not to owe him too many truths.

"How do you know the monster isn't me?" His eyes darkened, the left one pitch-black while the other glimmered a deep emerald.

She knew it wasn't him. If he wanted to, he could. But if he *were* the monster, he would've killed her that night last winter, not helped her. That was the hope she clung to, anyway.

"Is it?" she tossed back.

Nyx narrowed his eyes. Finally, he said, "Ridding this realm of it is not within my control." His voice was hard, but difficult to read.

Aurora's mouth deepened into a frown. There had to be *something* he could do—at the very least, give her a hint of what the beast was. She had already lost her parents; she didn't want to lose anyone else.

Her parents would want her to keep her siblings safe. But how could she keep them safe if she didn't know what she was protecting them from?

A tear slipped down her cheek. Max and Leila needed her. She had to do something to make their lives safer.

"But I can keep you safe," he whispered, his voice thick. She looked up at him, and his eyes were fixed on her cheeks—on the tears that ran down them. "That, I can do."

He cleared his throat and stood, then reached down to help Aurora to her feet, too. Any emotion she heard had vanished, his eyes vacant as he stared down into the flames below. Dread pitted in her gut and worry sank heavily against her chest. She didn't know what frightened her more—his tenderness or his ability to shut it off as if it were never there.

Before she could clear her mind, he forged ahead.

"It's why I brought you here, to have a safe place to come to when you need it." His gaze moved to hers. "The wood is not safe—especially past the curfew your village has put in place. Come here instead; you need only to ask when you're at the centermost point of

Lac Noir. The raven will guide you, and your wagon will have what you need when you return."

She blinked as his words sank in. He wanted her to come back. He didn't outright say it, but she could feel the longing that slipped into his words—the loneliness.

"Will there be a time I see you more than just in my dreams and in here?" she asked.

Not that she *minded* seeing him there, but now that she thought about it, she hadn't seen him outside of those two places. Even the Celestial Plane almost seemed to be *his* dreamworld more than a corporeal place.

"That is unlikely," he said simply.

Aurora's eyes narrowed, trying to gauge his response. His gaze guarded, he looked away from her.

"If you don't feel welcome, I wouldn't mind having you—"

"It isn't that," he interrupted. With his attention fixed on the stars, he said, "It's a curse of my blood."

Nyx's words were carefully chosen, slow and deliberate. As if each one held more weight than any he had said up until this point.

The question—how could a *god* be cursed?—sat on the tip of her tongue, but she held it back.

"A curse," she repeated, careful to phrase it as a statement rather than a question.

A muscle ticked in his jaw. "All magic has a price, Aurora."

She shivered as her name left his lips. The sound of it landed on her neck, trailing down and settling low on her spine. It was an odd feeling, a tingling sensation that left her wanting to hear him say it again.

His gaze flicked down to her mouth briefly—so quick she almost missed it—before snapping back up. "You need to go back now," he said abruptly. "Time passes differently here, but you should return."

"You still have two truths to ask." She didn't care that she was certain it was one more than she owed him, but she wasn't ready to leave. Being near him...it felt like a lifeline to her parents. Just like the carving. It was as if she were with them again, calling on the God of Fear and Dreams. Except this time, he answered back.

As soon as the thought crossed her mind, her chest tightened.

His face softened at her words, unknowing of the storm raging inside of her, the thin line of his mouth loosening as he watched her. "Perhaps I'll find you in your dreams."

She blinked, and when she opened her eyes, she found herself back in the middle of the frozen lake.

The fog had lifted, and just as Nyx had promised, her wagon was resting beside her. Her lips parted as she saw it was nearly overflowing. Clothing, bread, cheeses, and furs filled the cart—more than she had ever brought back in a whole lunar phase combined.

She slipped her hand into her pocket to grab her wooden carving, only to find it empty. She huffed a laugh and shook her head. He was so careful with her—almost as if he cared about her.

Fourteen

Nyx

The Divine were fucking with him. They had to be. Xenos had always been a bastard, eager to play tricks on gods and fae alike. Aurora *had* to be planted by someone to distract Nyx.

Nyx had already said too much—had already revealed more about the curse than he should have. It was more of nature's loophole to the gods existing than it was a curse, but he considered it just that all the same.

It had been so long since he had talked with a fae—so many years since he had been seen. He may have watched them for centuries, but nothing compared to what it felt like *speaking* with one.

Especially one like Aurora.

It made it impossible not to be intrigued by her—if only a little—not when it was only those who had a deep and true trust in *him* that made it possible for them to see him.

Even if his curse left him to only see her in her dreams, it would be enough.

Because he had to see her again, no matter in what capacity. She was the only fae that had been able to see him in *decades*. That had to mean something, and he intended to find out what.

Aurora had already proved her trust in him. She didn't run away screaming when he showed her his home—not even with the flames. He had taken her to another *world*, and yet she explored it with wide-eyed curiosity.

He had never shared his home with another before, never brought someone to a place so sacred and personal. But he had to. He had to give her a place in which she could seek safety. She didn't know the things that lurked just outside of her village, the monsters that crept so near to where she slept.

As much as he wished to lie to himself that he didn't care what happened to her, deeper thoughts tried to surface. But he shoved them down, refusing to make sense of the jumbled emotions prickling at his mind.

Nyx huffed a laugh and sat down on one of the cracked benches in his home.

Then his eyes widened, and he jolted back up. There should have been a large crack running down the length of the seat, one he hated to sit on but was unable to fix. No matter how hard he tried, the moment he would mend it, it would just break once more.

His temple used to be glorious, bathed in starlight during a never-ending night. In its prime, there wasn't a room left unkempt. The walls were lined with strings of fresh garland, and plush rugs lay across the floor.

But that was when people still prayed to him. *Believed* in him.

Emotions he had long abandoned nipped at his chest, a dull, aching pain that he had since turned to hate. Nyx had years of practice ignoring this feeling, and yet it rapped against his heart with a faint tap.

It stirred up forgotten desires, too. A time when he yearned for the joy fae felt when they heard his name.

Nyx swallowed as that faint tap began to pierce deeper into his chest. Memories of the early days when fae lost hope in him began to flood his thoughts, reminding him of why he abandoned those who first forsook him.

The steps at the entrance were the first to go, now uneven and covered in weeds. It was slow, like a flower one didn't notice wilting until it was too late to be saved. Then came the garland decaying, ivy taking over in all the rooms and across the walls. He tried to burn it off, but it reappeared within seconds.

He missed his ornately structured temple, once brimming with colorful stained-glass windows and jewel-lined doorways. But it had weathered millennia ago, just like he had.

It wasn't just a home; it was an extension of him.

He leaned in closer to examine the bench, finding the crack had sealed. It hadn't been in proper condition in…a century, maybe two. And yet it had been made whole without him doing anything to it.

But it didn't matter if one bench was fixed, or even if the ivy was eventually removed. This place would never be made whole.

Fifteen

Aurora

Aurora wiped the sleep from her eyes as someone banged against her bedroom door. The morning sun had come too soon, and that knocking was *far* too loud.

A strand of her hair was stuck to her cheek with dried drool. She hadn't slept this hard in ages.

"Aurora, it's midday!" Leila whined. "Max and I had to do our lesson without you today."

She groaned and rolled over, finding Max's bed empty. A painful weight of guilt settled on her chest at seeing him already gone. It was rare for her to miss their lessons, even if she was sick.

"Coming," she mumbled.

By the time she washed up and got dressed, Leila was unpacking the wagon.

"You went to the post too?" Aurora asked, the guilt sinking even more heavily in her stomach.

Leila rolled her eyes, unloading an armful of meats and cheeses. "I told you I can go by myself now." She lifted her arms, showing how much she had traded for—though Aurora suspected that was partly Nyx's doing. That was far more than they should've been able to trade for in the dead of winter. "You've been caring for us since we lost Mother and Father, so let us help you now that we can."

The front door swung open, and Max strolled through, a bundle of wood stacked in his arms. "And I got the firewood taken care of!" he said proudly.

Aurora chuckled and shook her head.

She spent the afternoon with her siblings, discussing plans for the future and how the village was far too small for Max and Leila. Aurora couldn't remember the last time she felt this relaxed—certainly not since she lost her parents.

As she lay in bed that evening, she couldn't help but send a silent prayer to Nyx, thanking him for what he had done for her family. Their pantry was overflowing, their clothes were fresh and warm, and they had everything they needed.

The more she thanked him—silently in her room without him to answer back—the more she wished she was with him to be able to see his reaction. To see if any flicker of emotion roared to life in his guarded eyes.

She grew restless, unable to fall asleep long after Max's soft snores filled the room. It wasn't long before she was lacing her boots up and slinging her furred coat on.

Nyx said she could go to the lake any time and be taken to his temple, and that was exactly what she intended to do.

***

The fog swept over the lake the moment Aurora asked to be taken to the temple, just as Nyx had said. Her raven arrived, swooping low and circling her, as if happy to see her, before leading her to the strange forest.

As chilly as the air was, she felt warmth fill her chest with every step she took. A smile tugged at her lips, drawing her feet into a quick pace.

She followed her raven through the odd trees until the lake disappeared behind her, not stopping when the crumbling stairs came into view. The raven cawed above her as it disappeared into the temple, and she ran after it with a smile on her face.

Being in the temple calmed Aurora. It brought her pulse to a rhythm so steady that she felt the heaviness of sleep press behind her eyes.

She wandered through the dark hallway, her footsteps quiet as she entered the main room.

It wasn't long before she found herself sitting on the bench upon which her wooden star had appeared the first night she came.

A warmth settled over her skin, the temperature that of a spring evening instead of a frigid winter night. She could feel a soft breeze on her face, lulling her to sleep.

She remembered wanting to see him, to give him a proper thank-you for everything he had given her family. But sleep called out to her, a temptress she couldn't refuse.

The last thing she remembered was leaning her back against the cool stone wall as her prayers to Nyx turned into a blissful slumber.

Sixteen

Nyx

Nyx watched her as she slept, her eyes closed and mouth relaxed.

The way her raven hair spilled across the stone was like a river of night cascading down a mountainside. It looked torturously soft, though it was frizzed at the ends and a few leaves had gotten tangled within the never-ending strands.

His fingers itched to pluck the leaves out, but he couldn't wake her. Not when she looked this peaceful. Instead, his gaze worked its way to her face, focusing on the gentle slope of her nose, the curve of her mouth and the faint smile that lay there.

She had fallen asleep on the very bench that had mended itself—a coincidence that didn't escape him. Even some of the ivy that used to be wrapped around the bottom had vanished, though he could've sworn it had been there before she sat down.

He didn't think she would want to come back here, to this crumbling building he called home. But she had. Not only did she come back, but she came back the very night after he had shown her.

The more Nyx watched Aurora, the more he realized that her

heart was just as beautiful as she was. A fae's heart was a curious thing, often fickle and selfish. Though he supposed the Divine were partly to blame for that—they were the most selfish of all.

But Aurora was different. The way that she cared for her siblings when their parents were taken away from them, how she put them before herself in every aspect of her life—even if she *deserved* to be selfish sometimes. She never chose to be. All that she had was theirs.

Nyx had heard it in her prayers, in her pleas for *their* safety and *their* health. He felt it in the way she focused on them, never on herself.

He had come to always expect the worst in the beings that plagued the realm—he still did. It drove him to a place of solitude, ignoring the realm and its constant begging for *more, more, more.*

Then there was Aurora.

Nyx found that he *wanted* to tell her about his life—his curse. He had never desired like this before, the feeling uncomfortable and itchy beneath his skin. Gods didn't *desire*. He shouldn't feel this way.

And yet he did.

This small spark of desire was swirling inside of him, refusing to dim. He supposed it had been there for some time, growing since the night he saved Aurora from the ignavis.

He had this desire to know more, while she had...hope.

That's what was different about her.

Warmth filled his chest as he watched her sleep, her face so peaceful and soft.

Aurora had *hope* in him.

There was this undeniable hope within her, one that sprouted from her belief in him. He had forgotten what it felt like to have someone believe in him.

That's why Aurora could see him when no one else could. Nyx didn't want to let himself think that was possible again. But here she was, in a place no one had ever been but him.

It *almost* made him want to believe in himself again.

So much so that he found he couldn't take his eyes off of her. Without thinking of the possible consequences, he joined her in her dreams.

Seventeen

Aurora

Aurora knelt beneath a worn oak tree in the wood. Her dreams were bringing her here more lately. Her limbs were heavy, and the breeze was warm, as if it were a spring morning. She hadn't meant to fall asleep in the temple, but she supposed praying here would do.

But this wood was slightly different than the real one, the darkness replaced by a soft golden glow along the forest floor. The blanket of snow emitted the dull light, brightening the world around Aurora from beneath her while the stars shone from above.

It left no room for darkness—an eternal illumination within the midst of night.

"I imagine your bed would be far more comfortable than the bench you fell asleep on." Nyx's warm voice floated over to her.

She raised her head and looked over her shoulder, not hearing him approach.

He was standing so close, she could smell his ice and freshly ground pepper scent. Tonight, he wore a simple black cotton buttondown, the sleeves pushed up to his elbows. His pants were the same, soft and dark.

Something in his relaxed appearance made butterflies dance in her stomach.

"You're in my dreams again," she breathed, looking up at him.

Nyx bent down and pushed her hair aside, tucking a few strands behind her ear. Heat crackled across her skin where his fingers brushed. Her mind went blank at the touch, and she felt as if lightning had struck her body, bringing a painful awareness to each and every nerve.

Aurora's eyes widened as her magic responded to his nearness—it answered of its own will, something it had never done before. She met his gaze, and there was something sparking beneath his split-colored irises, an amusement that danced across his face.

His mouth curved up. Something about him wasn't the same tonight. She couldn't help but notice the way he smiled—so different from the grim frown he wore when they met. There was a darkness in the curve of his lips, one that spoke of mischief rather than joy.

Suddenly, Nyx blinked rapidly, and the mirth in his eyes dissipated as if it hadn't been there at all. Before she could make sense of his abrupt change, he stepped away, leaving the warm breeze to flow between them as if they were two mountains separated by a deep valley.

"I didn't mean to fall asleep," she finally said, hoping to break the strange, uncomfortable tension that had formed between them.

Nyx blew out a breath, looking far more fae than god tonight. His features were those of the fae, but the otherworldly *feel* that surrounded him had softened. More than that, he wasn't as unnaturally stiff—his shoulders more relaxed and face soft.

"Dreams are better, anyway," he said lightly.

She grinned, finding that to be true on occasion. In truth, these days she slept so she could see him—living in her dreams more than she did in reality.

If only she could wrap her family up and take them to her dreams, too.

"But they can get lonely," she argued.

He gave her a sad smile. "*But* they're more fun."

She opened her mouth to protest that everything was more fun when friends or family were there to enjoy life with, but he stepped closer and offered his hand.

"Let me show you something." This time, she didn't hesitate to slip her hand into his. "Close your eyes."

She did as he asked, wiggling her feet in anticipation. The air cooled around her, a soft breeze brushing against her cheeks. Her body felt lighter, almost as if she were floating.

"Very good," he praised. "Now, open."

Her lashes fluttered open. Thousands of stars winked at her, twinkling closer than if she were standing on top of the tallest mountain in Zenovia.

She gasped when she looked down, realizing it wasn't a mountain she was standing on, but a *cloud*.

Nyx floated over to another cloud, close enough to talk but not enough to touch. He settled onto his, sitting on the edge and dangling his legs off the side. She followed suit, opting to lie down on hers, though the cloud was only big enough for her to roll once to either side.

"Much more fun than reality," he whispered, more to himself than to her. A wistful sigh left his lips, one she didn't think he meant to release.

He still managed to surprise her each time they were together, doing things that seemed far out of character for him. Perhaps that's why he always looked so uncomfortable.

"When are you going to ask me for the two truths?" she asked.

A small smile danced across Nyx's face, and he turned toward the other clouds. He was still stiff and oddly formal with her most of the time, but not tonight. "I'll ask when it's time," he answered vaguely. When he turned back to Aurora, there was a playful gleam in his eye. And then another smile.

She had asked another question.

"Before you say it," she blurted, "it doesn't count when the question is regarding the rules of the deal."

He never said she couldn't add more rules, but that didn't mean he would go for it.

Tonight, his green iris shone brighter than the midnight one. It almost seemed to bleed into his other eye, the navy mixing with emerald.

"Fine," he said with a small huff of laughter. "You'll likely ask me something once or twice before you wake up, anyway."

She *almost* asked how he was so confident in that, but caught herself before she did. Instead, she shook her head and laughed too. This deal was trickier than she thought it would be.

They were quiet for a moment, the dream realm peacefully comfortable. Aurora adored being in her dreams, but it was different with Nyx here. Less lonely in a way she didn't realize it had been before.

She positioned her hands behind her head as she stared up at the stars above them, the cloud beneath her back plush. "It's nice having you here," she whispered.

The moment she spoke, she realized how hollow that word was. *Nice.* It was more than nice; it was more than she should probably feel.

Nyx didn't respond, which wasn't a surprise. But then she heard a rustle and felt the aura of his presence move closer. She held her breath, careful to keep her eyes fixed above so he didn't change his mind.

The moment she felt him get closer, she couldn't resist looking. She turned her head, her back still pressed against soft but solid vapor.

He floated beside her, his arms resting on the cloud. She could only see him from the chest up, the rest of his body hidden.

From this angle, he was eye level with her—a position she realized she enjoyed because she could see his gaze so clearly. Could see the unspoken words written across his normally controlled face.

There was a question in his gaze, a hesitancy that she hadn't seen before. The longer she looked into his eyes, the more she realized what it was: vulnerability.

It made her feel closer to him, like she could see deeper than he meant to show her.

The air was thick between them—tense.

He drew back, as if sensing what she had seen. Quickly, she looked back up at the sky, hoping he wouldn't go.

Aurora wanted to say something, but no words came to mind, no thoughts to cling to.

Suddenly, she felt him lean closer, the chill of his presence pressing in.

"Am I what you imagined me to be?" he asked softly.

She shivered as his breath skittered across her cheek. It took her a moment to answer, her words caught in her throat once more. More than anything, she needed to see him—to gauge what small emotions she could find in his expression for the unspoken words he often kept hidden.

Something in his voice was off. Quiet.

Without thinking, she turned toward him again. This time, she angled her entire body, rolling over until her gaze met his.

Only it wasn't his gaze she met—it was the tip of his nose. Her nose bumped into his, and her entire body blazed a crimson-red. He seemed to be just as shocked, his body going deathly still.

The fire that trailed down her spine in the temple returned with vigor. It left a blazing path in its wake as it threatened to swallow her whole.

She had never been this close to him before... She found it wasn't close enough.

He cleared his throat and put an arm's length of distance between them, breaking the spell.

In truth, he was nothing like she imagined him to be. First, because she hadn't *imagined* him to be someone she would ever meet, let alone talk to. And second, she never pictured a god to be so...

faelike. But, more than anything, she hadn't imagined him to be so beautiful. Painfully and terribly beautiful.

The way his hair slightly curled along the nape of his neck, or how each muscle in his face was perfectly controlled. And his eyes... She loved that she always knew it was him just from those alone.

"You're nothing like I imagined you to be," she admitted. Nyx tilted his head to the side, and he leaned closer, eager for more. "Less terrifying."

His nose scrunched slightly as he said, "I can be terrifying."

It was almost too easy. He didn't seem to pick up on jokes quite like a fae or human would—didn't really seem to pick up on most emotions.

"It's a joke." She reached out and poked his arm, her chest lighter than it had felt in ages. "One truth gone and one left," she added.

His face relaxed instantly, as if he was worried she *would* think of him as terrifying. She should have been more afraid of him, but she wasn't. In fact, she wanted to be around him more. If she could, she would spend all day and every dream with him, asking him what it was like to be a god and why he didn't interact with people of the realm more.

People might think differently of him if they met him. He wasn't a horrifying creature eating fae and drinking their fear. What was light without darkness? Pain without pleasure? He was the hope of a dream while also being fear, a balance that relied on the other being there.

"What is it?" he asked slowly. "Your mouth is all scrunched to the side."

She instantly relaxed her lips, and her entire face flushed. "I was just thinking about how if the villagers met you, then they wouldn't be so afraid. Maybe even not call you a dark god—"

Lightning cracked in the distance, and his eyes darkened. He pulled away, floating back to the cloud he'd first occupied, which was a healthy ten paces away.

"I will always be who I am, Aurora." His voice was rough. Angry.

"That has not changed since the day fae were created and will remain until long after they're gone. Do not mistake me for something I am not."

If she hadn't been looking at him, she might have believed his words. But she *was* looking. She saw the torrent of self-loathing that swirled in his gaze—the way his expression shuttered and his brows drew together. His power pulsed off of him in waves.

She swallowed. "I don't believe you," she whispered, her words soft but firm. "You may not see it, but I do. You are *good*, Nyx."

The muscles in his jaw feathered. His eyes were darker—the midnight one now blacker than death, and the green one nearly matching it.

"Good night, Aurora," he finally said.

She wasn't ready to leave yet. "Wait—"

He paused, waiting for her to say something. She racked her brain for something to keep the conversation going and grabbed onto the first thing that came to mind.

"You gave me my carving back," she managed to say. "After you took it."

His gaze flickered, but he gave no indication that she was right.

She raised a brow, daring him to say something. It wasn't *quite* a question, but she wanted an answer all the same.

Nyx sighed and said, "I don't think the god you pray to would be terribly disappointed if you prayed without it."

Aurora's eyes widened, and she stared at him. "Did you just... make a joke?"

He tilted his head to the side, and a small smile played across his face. Just like that, the tension dissipated between them. "I suppose I did."

Once again, Aurora almost forgot that the being before her wasn't fae.

"Fast learner," she muttered with a grin.

His gaze was so curiously open, as if he had surprised himself, too. She could look into his eyes and never grow tired of it, could study the bright green beneath the sunlight and the midnight-blue under the glow of the moon.

There were small crinkles at the corners of his eyes, his smile soft.

It made her want to know him more—the parts he kept hidden and the ones he hadn't shown anyone. She wondered if he felt the same way.

Eighteen

Aurora

Aurora waited patiently as Nyx floated up, sitting beside her on a cloud of shadows that he had conjured. She sat up too, mirroring his position with his feet dangling over the edge as he had earlier. She on her white, puffy one, and he on his dark, shadowy creation.

"I'd like to know more about your curse," she said hesitantly.

Nyx glanced at her, and she met his gaze, holding it until the silence stretched too far past comfort and she squirmed beneath the look in his eyes. He was watching her closely, searching her face as if he were an artist studying a painting—uncertain if he liked what he saw.

"Each of the gods has a...restriction to their power," he whispered. Her brows shot up, surprised that he had said anything at all. "Mine is why I haven't seen you outside of your dreams or the Celestial Plane."

Shock rippled through her at the direct answer. He hadn't been the most forthcoming with things that dealt directly with him—unsurprising, given he was a god. She didn't know what made him suddenly open up, but if he was willing to talk, then she was more than happy to listen.

"So your curse is..." Her voice trailed off, unable to place the words.

"Nature's loophole," he finished with a nod.

The information sank in, and things started to make more and more sense.

"So, the night you saved me?" she asked.

A small grin formed on his lips. Her eyes tracked the movement, a smile working its way onto her mouth in return.

"I was there, but you could not see me," he explained. "No one has been able to see me for decades."

Her mouth scrunched to the side as she thought. "Until me?"

"Until you," he murmured, more to himself than to her. "I didn't think the time would come for a fae to see me again."

But she *had* seen him. The night when only his eyes appeared after she had been saved by him, then again in her dreams the night she fell asleep with the star in her hand, and often since.

"Why *me?*" she asked quietly. "What changed?"

Another smile appeared on his face, one she found herself watching once again. A small breeze rustled his hair and caused strands to fall into his eyes. He didn't move to fix it, but her fingers itched to reach up and do it for him.

She blinked a few times, trying to center her thoughts.

"You did." His eyes bore into her, bright and curious. "The curse...it's dependent on someone believing in me—a true and with-out-falter kind of belief."

Aurora's breath caught. She could remember that night so clearly; the way the shadows appeared, too strong to be conjured by any ordinary fae. They had appeared just after she prayed to Nyx directly, desperate for an answer. The whole way home, she chanted her gratitude to him, her thoughts already turning away from the other gods and focusing on him alone.

She couldn't fall asleep at first, her heart still hammering in her chest after the attack. So, she stayed awake, chiseling Nyx's symbol onto a square block with a small inscription beneath it.

Now that she thought about it, she hadn't seen that carving in ages—so different from the small star she'd kept beneath her bed for the last few seasons.

Once she was done carving, she had calmed enough to fall asleep. At which point she found Nyx's eyes awaiting her in her dreams.

Then, the night when she fell asleep with her star in her hand, her thoughts had been set on him. And he'd found her in her dream-world again, this time whole.

But if she had been the only one able to see him...

"What about everyone else?" she asked. "There has to be someone else that believes as strongly as I do. Luca prayed to all the Divine—you included."

"Luca believed in the Divine as a whole—a unit. He didn't pray to *me*; he prayed as if we were one. The strength of his belief wasn't like yours. It was..." Nyx shook his head and let his gaze fall to where his hands rested on his knees. His voice lowered as he whispered, "There is no one but you, Aurora."

She swallowed, her breathing shallow. "So, if the curse requires me to believe in you to see you in my dreams, what has to happen for me to see you in the waking realm?"

His eyes briefly closed, as if to hide whatever emotion he didn't want her to see. She had already asked him so many questions that she probably owed him twenty truths. But she would keep asking as long as he continued to answer.

"A bloodletting," he answered softly. Nyx opened his eyes and turned to look at her. "To be corporeal in the waking realm, to walk among the dirt as the fae do, and for you to see me, there's only one thing I have to do," he said quietly, his voice steady. "I would need to drink the blood of a willing participant."

Her mouth parted upon hearing the last word out of his mouth. The words *drink the blood* bounced throughout her mind, spinning around and around. She tried to make sense of it.

"You—"

"I think that's enough for tonight," he said quickly. "Good night."

Before Aurora could say anything more, she was plunged into darkness. Her eyes snapped open, and she found herself back in her cottage, no longer lounging on a cloud but in a stiff bed.

Aurora wasn't hurt that he cut their dream off; she knew he wasn't trying to upset her. He was *afraid*. She could see through the abrupt halt in their conversation—the pain and fear that hid there.

She wasn't afraid of him. Shocked by his words, yes, but not afraid. As much as he might have thought his confession about the bloodletting would frighten her, he couldn't be further from the truth. Aurora was *curious*. She had never heard of anyone needing to feed on one's blood to sustain their magic.

And if he needed a willing participant...

She shivered at the possibilities. At the excitement that filled her.

Nyx had saved her last winter; the least she could do was offer him something in return.

But Nyx was afraid of her seeing who he really was. She knew he wasn't all good—no one was. He was dark, and he was light. He was the sun, and he was the moon.

And one day, she would make sure everyone knew it.

Nineteen

Nyx

The days bled into weeks, the winter growing harsher with each passing day. It kept the villagers in their homes, sitting in front of hearths with thick furs wrapped around them.

But it gave Nyx time to see Aurora.

Ever since she looked him in the eye and swore she saw good in him, he couldn't help but be curious *why* she thought that. He had been called many things, but never good.

Not to mention that he had told her something he hadn't told anyone before. His curse was personal—like standing in front of someone completely naked, body and soul bared to them.

He was certain she would stop praying to him after he had told her the truth behind his curse. Convinced she would come to her senses and find a new god—a better one—to believe in. Then perhaps he would fade into nothing, becoming a footnote in history texts and forgotten generations from now. It was likely better that way, more suitable for Aurora to place her trust in a good god, like Astoria—kind and gentle. Or Celeste, wise and strong.

But just as she had the night they lay on clouds, she returned to him.

She hadn't brought up their conversation since the night he told her, and for that he was grateful. He needed time to adjust to someone else knowing, time for him to process *why* he had told her in the first place.

He could've easily told her a lie, or given a non-answer. But she believed in him enough for them to be there in the first place; the least he could do was be honest in return.

The more she came to Lac Noir and called out to him, the more comfortable he grew around her. He would send his raven to meet her and bring her to his realm, where they would find a place to talk—sometimes sitting beneath the stars, while other times they walked through the temple or on the grounds around it.

It became such a common meeting that he would send his raven to wait on her, knowing she would show up on the icy lake. He would watch her through the bird's eyes, warmth growing in his chest as her flushed cheeks and pink nose came into view.

Their conversations grew longer, often lasting until just before the sun rose.

Tonight, they sat atop Nyx's temple, bathed in moonlight and the glow of the stars. The roof was half-crumbling, but they had found a small intact section on the edge. Nyx let his feet dangle, his legs swaying gently back and forth, while Aurora leaned against a corner pillar.

"You're doing that on purpose," she said softly.

He had avoided looking at her this evening, certain that he would get lost in her gaze if he did. So, he kept his eyes on the sky as he said, "Doing what?"

Out of the corner of his eye, he saw her point in the direction of the forest. She had asked *several* times what the limit of this realm was, how far it went, and what lay beyond. He never knew how to answer—how to explain that it rested in between reality and dream, a mixture of chaos and order.

"The trees are rustling to the rhythm of your feet." Her voice was soft—curious. He lowered his gaze, watching as a soft breeze followed the movements of each foot. The left side billowed away from him as that foot swung out, the right side bending toward him as that leg came in.

"Or does it just happen?" she asked.

He smiled at her curiosity and her question. "You really can't help yourself, can you?" he muttered to himself and shook his head. "So eager to give up your truths? You should be far more careful, Aurora."

Before she could answer, he continued, a thrill running through him at getting to ask her for another truth. "The place is an extension of me," he explained. "This temple, those trees...they're a part of me. I don't intend for magic to happen here, but it does. It happens as easily as breathing—you don't realize you're doing it, but it happens nonetheless. Just as your heart pumps blood and your lungs expand with air. Each is vital for the body to survive, but all with a different job."

She hummed and said, "So you need this place as much as it needs you."

A small smile worked its way onto his face. The clever little fae was catching on, careful not to ask questions—though not getting to play their game left a hollow ring in his chest.

"In a way, yes." He realized it was one of the most honest conversations he'd had in decades. He didn't interact with fae or humans often; his companions were limited to the gods, so he could either enjoy their company or spy on mortals—which was why he chose to spend most nights alone.

He never realized how lonely it was until Aurora. Many of his evenings were now filled with her standing in the center of Lac Noir, the ice beneath her feet and snow falling in her hair as she called out to him.

It was odd to think that there was someone out there who wanted to see him as much as he wanted to see her.

He would have been suspicious of her intentions, had she not been the one to see him when no one else could.

The thing was, she didn't *want* anything from him. There was no ulterior motive, no scheme being concocted to steal his power. But that was all he knew. Vidaris craved power more than any of the other gods, but they all had knives in their hands, hidden behind their backs as they smiled. That's just how the gods were—how *he* was.

But with Aurora, he hadn't thought about those things. Hadn't been plagued with thoughts of what Vidaris could be up to or what Xenos was planning. With Aurora, he was just...present. Content. An escape he didn't know he needed, let alone wanted.

Nyx cleared his throat, feeling an uncomfortable ache in the center of his chest. "You asked your question, now I get a truth," he said. She snorted softly, knowing he would always bring it back to their deal. "But I want you to choose which truth you give this time, no matter how big or small. You choose."

It was still within the confines of their bargain; she could ask him a question, and if he answered, he got a truth from her in return. This time, he wanted her to decide what she revealed.

"Even if it's just telling you about my favorite blanket from when I was a child?" she teased.

He could hear the grin in her voice, but he kept his eyes fixed firmly on the stars as he nodded and said, "Even then."

Aurora was quiet for a moment, likely thinking of ways to tell him about her favorite...blanket. Even though he didn't fully understand how one could have an attachment to such a thing.

"Leila wants to explore the realm, maybe see the palace or sail the seas," she began softly. He saw her reposition herself out of the corner of his eye, pulling her legs to her chest and wrapping her arms around them. "That used to be me, before our parents died."

Her words sent a shiver through his body. It was more than he expected her to give him—far more. She was choosing this not because he had asked it or because of their bargain, but because she *wanted* to.

What right did he have to see this piece of her soul?

When she sniffled lightly, he couldn't keep his gaze from finding hers. Just as he suspected, her eyes matched the glow of the moon. Bright and hauntingly familiar, a blue so pale it shone more silver in certain lights.

Their gazes collided, but he couldn't read the emotion behind hers.

He found himself asking, "What changed?"

Aurora blinked, the emotion whirling in them dimming slightly. "Me," she whispered. "My life became taking care of Leila and Max. I don't resent them for it, but it changed me. I was trying to figure out how to survive on my own while also having to make sure *they* survived, too. Not just survived, but lived—truly lived. Teaching them, feeding them until they were old enough to help, being their sole provider..."

She blew out an unsteady breath, her gaze growing distant.

"But they're older now," Nyx said gently. "You can still leave when they've grown to be independent."

It seemed easy enough with how old Leila was now and with Max not far behind. Aurora could be anything she wanted to be, could go anywhere she wished to go. And yet she still looked so sad.

"It's different now." Aurora rested her chin on her knees, her gaze dropping to where her boots poked out in front of her. "I threw my grief of losing my parents into taking care of my siblings. I was all they had, but *they* were also all that I had. If I could focus on taking care of them, I wouldn't have to face what I was feeling."

Nyx swallowed and clenched his teeth together. Gods weren't in tune with their emotions as fae or humans were. And yet he understood this.

A tear slipped down her cheek, and while he didn't know how to help her, he knew he didn't want to see her hurt.

He reached toward her and swiped his thumb over the tear, brushing it away. Instead of pulling his hand away, he let his knuckles graze down her cheek and settle under her chin. He tilted her face up, his gaze searing into hers.

"You're afraid of what happens when they leave," he whispered.

She nodded, his grip still lightly grasping her chin. "They won't need me anymore."

He had never heard her sound so broken. All Nyx knew was that he wanted to comfort Aurora. He wanted to take her pain away and shield this perfect woman from the cruelty of the world around her.

Aurora had done *so much* for her family, had sacrificed her aspirations and dreams for them. Yet here she was, the wound of all she had dealt with still freshly opened on her heart.

He didn't know much by way of consoling others, but when he had held her the day she first came to his home, it had seemed to help. It was a knee-jerk reaction that night, something he had seen fae and humans do countless times.

Her heartbeat slowed when he wrapped his arms around her. He didn't know if he had done it right, but he mirrored what he saw others do. If it helped her that night, then he would do it again and again.

Before he could think better of it, he swung his legs up onto the roof.

With his body facing hers, he whispered, "Come here."

Aurora only hesitated a moment before she obeyed. She melted into him, lying against his chest with her hands trembling as she rested them beneath her cheek.

Her body was soft against his, her flesh smooth and warm. Nyx was acutely aware of the way her weight felt against him, his nostrils flaring as he tried to focus. He wrapped his arms around her, hoping that if he could make her feel safe, he could chase the pain away.

But he knew it had to be more than this. That she didn't just need someone to hold her, but to let her know that she wasn't alone. And Nyx knew alone more than anyone.

"I don't know what it's like to have lived the life you've experienced," he whispered into her hair softly. "What I do know is that the realm is a cruel and selfish place. I thought humanity was damned—with people killing one another to gain power, stealing from those less fortunate, and more hate between fae and humans than ever before.

"But you, Aurora..." He tightened his arms around her. "You give me hope that the realm still has light within the darkness."

More than that—though he didn't say it aloud—she made him feel like the people of this realm might be worth saving after all.

"The carving," she breathed.

His brows drew together, trying to make sense of the change in subject. Perhaps he had said too much.

Aurora took a steadying breath and said, "The carving that I keep? It reminds me of my parents. It isn't just for you. It's for them—for the generations of women in my family that it has been passed down to. That's why I was so upset when it went missing." Her voice trembled, and his chest tightened as he scrambled for some way to soothe it.

But she continued, as brave as she was afraid. "Losing it was like losing them all over again. If I could see the stars, I was never truly alone—that's what she would say. But in my mind, it became seeing *that* star meant she was always with me—that the wooden carving was what kept her close. And that's why I couldn't part with it." Her words grew stronger with each breath. "But then you came along, and I realized what my mother meant. She meant *you* would be with me.

"Of course there would come a day I would be without her," Aurora continued. Though she spoke softly, he had never heard her sound so confident. "But she knew there would never be a day I would be without *you*."

She pulled away from him, something in her gaze flipping suddenly, like a fire roaring to life. There was a determination in her eyes unlike anything he had seen before. His arms flinched, muscles tightening as he braced himself for what she was about to say.

"Drink from me," she whispered, her voice soft but sure.

A whirring began to fill Nyx's ears. His body hummed to life at the words, vibrating with a need he hadn't felt in a long time.

He blinked, *certain* he hadn't heard her right. "Aurora—"

"Nyx." She reached for his hands, gripping them between her own. With the way she was looking at him, he had a growing suspicion he would do anything she asked of him. "*Drink* from me. I'm here, I'm willing. You said you had to drink the blood of a willing participant. Well, you have one. You have me."

Something new settled in his chest, a flicker of an emotion he hadn't felt before. He watched the way her dark hair fell down her shoulders in soft waves, the way her pale blue eyes matched the moon on a clear night.

Aurora was beautiful—so beautiful that it frightened him.

He didn't have a fear of not being able to control himself; all it took was a few sips.

In the past, he had a line of willing participants. There were temples in his name, inside of which texts filled with lore and history on him resided. Those who worshiped him would leave chalices filled with blood for him to imbibe as he pleased, an abundance at his disposal.

That was before they had begun to turn away from him. Before people started to call him, Xenos, and Vidaris the Triad of Dark Gods. Before they were afraid of him and cursed his name instead of praising it.

Even in all that time, he hadn't hungered for blood. It was simply a means to an end, nothing more and nothing less.

But Nyx *hungered* for Aurora.

He had only drunk directly from the vein a handful of times, opting to drink from the cups left for him instead. Bloodletting straight from fae could get...intimate. And there was nothing Nyx hated more than intimacy. He didn't want anyone to see that side of him, didn't want to be vulnerable.

But to do it with Aurora...

Warmth filled his body, spreading through his chest at the thought. He hadn't let himself consider it—didn't want to torment himself by obsessing over what it could be like.

Yet here she was, offering the very thing the darkest corners of his mind craved.

Aurora didn't know the full truth of his curse—didn't know the ins and outs of how each of the Divine was plagued with a different affliction. He didn't deserve her loyalty, her trust.

He didn't deserve any of this.

"Nyx," she said gently, pulling his thoughts back to the hauntingly beautiful woman in front of him. "I wouldn't offer it if I didn't mean it."

He breathed out a deep sigh, his thoughts running in a thousand different directions. "A bloodletting in this way isn't as simple as you think." He cleared his throat, his voice gravelly and deep. "Drinking directly from you would be...an experience. Your body would respond to it, and the pull is quite strong."

Of course, that's just what he had been *told* by the few he had drunk from—quick, purposeful encounters. He felt something similar when he drank from the cup: a rush of power filling his veins, as if the chains tampering with his magic were suddenly released.

But nothing compared to drinking warm blood that still pumped through the body.

"I can handle it," Aurora whispered. She leaned closer to him, her hands still resting in his. His eyes widened as she swept her long hair over to one shoulder, exposing her neck to him. "Let me do this for you."

Nyx kept his attention fixed firmly on her face while a war raged inside of him.

There shouldn't have been any hesitancy—Aurora was the solution to a problem he had given up on long ago. Here she was, offering herself so effortlessly, not a drop of doubt in her gaze.

So what made him pause?

It could be that Aurora was the most incredible creature he had ever seen. From the way her eyes rivaled the beauty of the moon, to the gentle scent of pine that clung to her hair. Or perhaps it was what she had shown tonight—that her kindness was greater than that of any other fae he had encountered.

Whatever the reason, he didn't want to hurt her. It may only take a few sips to get what he needed, but the rush of power that accompanied the bloodletting was...often intoxicating.

And he had never been this long without drinking. Who was to say he would even be able to stop himself from draining her body entirely?

"I don't want to hurt you," he whispered.

A memory flashed through his mind of a panicked young fae male. He had offered Nyx his arm, willing and unknowing to the fate that awaited him.

The fae's gaze had been filled with terror in those last moments. Glorious, euphoric power rushed through Nyx's veins as he drank from the fae. At first, the male was still and quiet. Until the blood began to drain to the last dregs and he realized Nyx wasn't going to stop. *Couldn't* stop.

Even as the male fought against Nyx's hold, he was no match for the god. A willing participant had been brought to an early grave, dead before Nyx could stop himself from draining his body entirely.

Not to mention that had happened even *with* regularly scheduled bloodletting.

It was the last time he had allowed himself to drink in that way. If he started to kill his followers, they would surely turn against him.

But it seemed fate had arranged for that to happen anyway.

Nyx swallowed, hoping Aurora would let this go.

"You need this," she said firmly as she leaned in closer. Her hands came up to his face, careful but sure. "Drink."

The command was fierce, stronger than anything Aurora had said to him before. It was the final thing to cause his resolve to snap.

Nyx's eyes drifted down to Aurora's neck, the midnight breeze rustling wisps of her hair across her skin.

Her hands fell away from his face, and he instantly wished they would return. It had been so long since someone believed in him this much.

He blew out a quick breath and slowly bent down toward her. With a gentle sweep, he brushed her hair out of the way, holding it over the other shoulder with one hand. With his free hand, he traced a path along her neck, his thumb lightly following along the curve of her shoulder.

"You're sure of this?" he asked a final time, his eyes briefly flicking up to meet hers.

She smiled—the sight breathtaking and drawing Nyx closer to her. "Quit stalling."

Nyx chuckled softly, his breath dancing across her skin and causing goosebumps to scatter in its wake.

He leaned forward until his lips brushed her neck. It was an odd gesture, a carefulness he didn't often exhibit with others. But it felt... right. And if he wanted to do right by anyone, it was the one person who had believed in him when no one else did.

"You are a difficult woman to say no to," he murmured against her skin.

She laughed, the sound breathy and uneven—the only sign of nerves she had shown thus far.

Without wasting another moment, he opened his mouth, allowing his teeth to rest against her flesh. She jumped, just slightly, and he gave her a minute to adjust to the sensation.

One of his hands still held her hair gently aside, while the other slid around to cup the back of her head.

He could feel her melt into him, and he knew she was ready.

Nyx's teeth sank into Aurora's neck.

The moment her blood touched his tongue, he couldn't stop the groan that rumbled from his throat. He may never see the light of Caelum, but he imagined it wouldn't compare to the way this felt.

A burst of power exploded through his veins, winding throughout his body and filling him with so much magic that it made his head light. He pressed his teeth harder against her, drawing more blood out.

Her hands shot to his shirt, twisting the fabric tightly and drawing him closer. He eagerly pulled her in deeper, the blood sweet and spicy at the same time.

The more he drank, the more his body craved it. Small whimpers slipped from her mouth, and he felt the vibration each time.

He knew she would be experiencing something similar to drinking a touch too much wine or smoking too much root. But what he wasn't prepared for was how he was experiencing the same thing.

It wasn't just a rush of power that filled him, but a need to have *her*. To mark her as his, to ensure no one else would know her the way he did. It was a primal feeling. Dark. He had no right to desire these things, and yet with each sip, the need intensified.

Nyx felt something wet dribble from the corner of his mouth and down his chin. He reached up with every intention to simply wipe it away. But then he felt how the blood had slipped onto her skin, trailing across her chest.

Intoxicated with the energy surging through him, he smeared the blood up and onto the front of her neck. His finger traced the column of her throat, following the swallow that worked its way down.

Her hand clenched his shirt tighter as her head began to loll. His hand held her upright, and he knew he should pull away—knew that it was time to stop.

But another breathy moan escaped her lips, and he found one stirring in his chest in answer.

"Nyx," she breathed.

Hearing his name on her lips made his head nearly as light as when he drank from her.

He wrenched himself off of her, a soft gasp coming from her lips when his teeth left her skin. His magic coursed through him, but it dulled the moment he leaned away.

From the corner of his eye, he saw her hand move toward him. His body went deathly still, his skin sensitive to even the lightest breeze.

Her thumb swiped beneath his lip, the metallic scent of blood filling the air. His nostrils flared in answer, and the hunger returned.

He opened his mouth—to say what, he wasn't sure—but she stopped him.

Aurora's thumb glided into his mouth, offering the last bit of blood to him. His tongue greedily met her finger and gently sucked it off.

A small moan slipped from her throat again.

It was what he needed to snap out of it. He pulled back, breaking their connection abruptly.

She sucked in a breath, her body shivering as he leaned away.

His eyes lifted to her neck, where blood still trickled from the mark he left. It wouldn't take long for her body to heal itself—a fae's healing was far more accelerated than a human's—but she shouldn't have to wait.

Slowly, he reached up and pressed his thumb to the small wound. Her pulse thumped against his touch, steady and quick. He swallowed, focusing on pushing his newly charged power into mending her flesh back together.

The mark disappeared as he swiped his thumb over it, the blood smearing but the wound vanishing entirely. As if it had never happened.

Nyx could still taste her. Could still feel the buzzing in his veins with the abundance of power flowing through them. His nostrils flared, his chest warm and body buzzing on every nerve ending.

He had never felt that way during a bloodletting before. Power, yes—but the warmth, the intensity and possessiveness... That was *very* different.

A part of him was afraid to look at her, to see fear replacing the trust that he usually found written across her face.

He braced himself and slowly lifted his gaze to meet hers.

Her eyelids were heavy, and her lips formed a lazy smile. "You didn't tell me it would feel like...that," she murmured.

The look in her eyes wasn't fear; it was content. It was a look that filled him with something dangerous: love.

Twenty

Aurora

Aurora settled into her bed, her thoughts content and body warm beneath a bundle of newly blanketed furs Nyx had stored in her wagon. He had given her enough for Max and Leila, too—something she would be eternally grateful to him for.

But she had given him something as well.

The bloodletting was unlike anything she had ever experienced. She had never felt more alive than when his teeth grazed her skin, sinking in and drawing not just blood, but unexpected pleasure.

It was warm and gentle, like a soft pulse that set her flesh aflame. She could feel him everywhere—not just the tender way he held her head or the gentleness when he pulled her hair to the side, but in her chest, her stomach...lower, even.

Aurora buzzed with excitement that she'd been able to give herself to Nyx. He had saved her, had given her family more goods than they needed, and brought her to his home. But Aurora only had herself.

She didn't expect to open up to him on the rooftop of his temple, but no one had ever asked her those questions before. Everyone in her life knew what happened to her parents, most of them having lost someone they loved, too.

It almost made it easy to forget other people's pain when one was so used to looking at it. It was even easier to forget that the pain was there.

Still, Nyx saw through her—through the façade, the smiles.

He was *gentle*. Kind. Even as she offered her blood to him, he had hesitated, worried he would hurt her. But she knew he wouldn't. She could see the determination in his eyes, a look that told her she was safe with him.

Maybe now she would get to see him outside of her dreams and the Celestial Plane. She should've asked how long it would take for the bloodletting to work—if she would see him soon.

Her body begged for sleep, exhausted from the night's events.

She sent him a quick prayer of thanks before her eyes got too heavy to keep open. The room around her was still and quiet, save for Max's light snores. He was always asleep the moment his head hit his feathered pillow—another gift from Nyx.

Time passed differently when she was with him in the Celestial Plane. It felt as if it should have been sunrise by the time she made it home, but the moon had hardly moved in the sky.

Just as she was about to drift into sleep, a buzzing filled the air. It started as a quiet hum but quickly grew so loud it nearly shook her bones. She slapped her hands over her ears, her vision wobbly from the fierceness of the sound. When she glanced at Max, he was still sound asleep.

She shook her head and stumbled out of bed. Fear spiked in her chest and squeezed her heart painfully. Her vision went black, and even though the cottage was dark at night, the hearth should have provided enough light to see by.

She blindly felt through the room, her hands running along the wall, hoping fresh air would lessen the piercing noise. After throwing on a coat and slipping into her thick boots, she flung herself outside.

Cold air blasted across her cheeks as the door clicked shut behind her. The buzzing receded enough for her to see, but the shapes of the trees were still blurry.

She took a few steps forward and found the sound to lessen a touch more. After taking a handful of steps away from the cottage again, it had quieted enough for her to stop shaking. But it was still on the cusp of unbearable, the weight of the noise propelling her further into the wood. And away from her cottage.

Away from her siblings.

But Max had been sound asleep, unaffected by what was happening to her.

If it was something happening only to her, she had to get away from there—couldn't pull them into whatever was hurting her. She had to put distance between herself and them; otherwise, they might feel it too.

So, she pushed her feet forward, stumbling step by step while chanting the names of her siblings to keep her going.

It wasn't until snow-covered pines and darkness surrounded her that the pain from the noise drifted into silence. The forest was so still, so quiet, that it nearly felt as loud as the awful buzzing.

Aurora pressed her hand over her racing heart, realizing now that she was in calf-deep snow and out past curfew. The moon was hidden by clouds, making the wood so dark she could hardly see which way to go.

She spun in a circle, willing herself to stay calm. If she panicked, she wouldn't find her way back. And if she didn't find her way back...

She shivered and pulled her coat tighter around her shoulders.

None of the trees around her looked familiar, so she picked a direction and started walking. As she walked, she cast her shadows out to all sides like a net, feeling her surroundings with them.

She could ask Nyx for help, but she didn't know what help he could give if the bloodletting hadn't set in yet. It wasn't the first time she had been out here after dark, but never this late. Perhaps she could just—

One of her shadows—the one stretching to the west—recoiled

suddenly. It sent a shock wave through her body as her magic slammed back into her. The feeling wasn't something she had felt before. It was dark, almost like death itself.

She spun and walked in the opposite direction, using her shadows like a small shield around her. Her magic wasn't strong enough to stave off a dark creature for long, but it was enough to give her time to run if she got lucky.

A panicked scream pierced the air from somewhere deep within the trees. It felt as if it was coming from every direction, the noise bouncing in a chamber of echoes around her, keeping her from pinpointing exactly where it was coming from.

She spun around, frantically trying to locate the cry. It was feminine, of that she was sure—the anguish-ridden octave piercing and sharp.

The scream abruptly stopped, and a deafening silence rang in Aurora's ears as her heart thundered against her rib cage. The hair on her neck and arms stood on end. She froze, her shadows recoiling back into her once more.

Aurora waited, ears straining to pick up any sound that didn't belong to the forest.

Just as a sinking sensation filled her stomach at the thought that she was unable to help whoever it was, the screech started up again, this time clearly coming from her left.

Someone was in trouble.

This time, she didn't hesitate to ask Nyx for his help.

Nyx, someone is in danger—and likely me soon. She nearly shouted the prayer in her mind. *If you can, please help—*

The scream rang out again, closer still, interrupting her thoughts. Her feet moved before she could think better of it, and she sprinted toward the sound.

Her feet pounded into the fresh snow, packing it down as she tore through the trees. As she ran, what was left of the buzzing disappeared entirely, replaced by the screams of a woman. She had to help

—she couldn't just leave someone to die. Nyx would be here any minute now.

Through the trees, she could see the outline of a woman crumpled to the ground. Her long, golden hair hung like a curtain over her face. She wore nothing but a thin, tattered white shift.

Aurora slowed to a walk as she approached, her eyes searching their surroundings for what could've caused the woman to be so afraid. But the forest was quiet.

"Are you hurt?" Aurora asked softly, careful not to get too close and scare her.

The woman's shoulders shook, her face pressed into the dirt and hidden by her hair. Soft cries followed Aurora's question.

"I won't harm you," Aurora added. "I'm here to help. Just tell me what you need."

The crying paused. The woman mumbled, too softly for Aurora to hear, so she stepped closer and crouched down in front of her.

Slowly, the woman raised her head, her hair trickling across her face to reveal her eyes. They were pitch-black—a soulless depth peering back.

Aurora gasped and fell backward, her feet tangling in roots covered by the snow. It made her feel the same way as whatever her shadows had touched. Like pure death.

The woman smiled and tilted her head to the side. She stood so quickly that Aurora barely had time to blink before she was towering over her.

"What are you?" Aurora breathed.

Instead of words leaving the woman's mouth, a screech came out. A sound so unnatural that it vibrated through every bone in her body.

Aurora crawled backward on her hands, the icy snow biting into her flesh. She couldn't look away from the creature, her eyes forced to watch as it stalked toward her.

Then, something caught her right wrist and yanked. She fell

back, her head slamming into the ground. Her ears rang and the base of her skull throbbed.

A slender rope-like thread snaked around her left wrist, then her right, pinning her arms to the ground. She kicked her legs frantically as it wound its way down her stomach and legs, before finally wrapping around her ankles too.

The thin rope continued across her entire body, winding around piece by piece. She couldn't look at the woman from this position, but she could hear her. The sound of cloth tearing and bones shattering filled the air.

Maybe Nyx had come to save her, maybe—

The ground shuddered beside her, followed by the crunch of snow. It sounded like eight sticks piercing the ground one by one instead of a pair of feet.

For the first time, Aurora began to doubt Nyx would come.

Maybe the bloodletting hadn't worked.

She struggled against the bindings, tossing her head up and side to side. Her arms were pinned to her sides, her legs wrapped together.

A white gleam caught her eye—the rope that held her down. Only it wasn't rope. It was white silk, the threads so thin that one ribbon seemed to be made of thousands of strands.

Aurora's heart stopped. It wasn't rope. It was a spider's web.

Something yanked on her ankles, dragging her across the ground. She bit back a scream, mind racing as she strained to find a way out of this. Her shadows gathered in her palms, but the moment they touched the sticky web, they bounced back toward her. As if she were trying to cut down a tree with a blade of grass.

Panic gripped her throat—her magic wouldn't work.

A rock that stuck up from the snow cut across her left shoulder, slicing through her coat and ripping it. Ice and rocks tore at her now-bare skin, and she bit her lip to keep her cries of pain at bay.

Trees blurred above her and slowly turned into a rocky mountainside. The creature was taking her somewhere—likely to kill her—

and she would do everything she could to get away from it. She thrashed her body side to side, trying to get the web caught on something sharp enough to cut it. But nothing worked. It was impenetrable.

She was dragged into a cavern, webs covering the ceiling. Not just webs—bones hung within them. Bones that had been cleaned until they were gleaming a pearly white. Just like the ones left over from the villagers who had gone missing.

This wasn't just a monster hiding in the wood—this was the very one that had been terrorizing her village for years.

She was going to die. Tonight was the night.

Nyx, if you can hear me, please come. She wasn't too proud to beg for his help; it was the only way out of this she could think of. But as the creature pulled her deeper into its cave, any hope of him saving her faded.

For once—possibly when it mattered the most—Nyx wasn't going to come.

Aurora's body was suddenly weightless. Her vision blurred as the world spun. The creature slammed her against a rock wall, sticking her in a woven mass of spun silk. She was positioned upright, but the cave was so dark, she could hardly see.

A clicking noise sounded from in front of her, moving closer with every rapid breath she took. She shook inside of the cocoon, chanting prayers to Nyx as the creature pressed in.

When she finally could see it, she knew she was going to die.

A thousand beady red eyes blinked at her, covering its massive head. The woman had vanished, replaced by what she feared it was: a spider three times her size.

This *thing* wasn't a woman at all, but some sort of shifter.

Saliva oozed from its mouth and dripped down the front of her cocoon. It burned its way down, sizzling on impact and heating her from the outside in.

Nothing could save her now.

The spider loomed over her, and she pressed her back into the rock, desperate to get away. But there was nowhere to go. She opened her mouth to scream, to beg—

The ruffle of feathers echoed through the cave, causing the creature to pause. A shudder ran through it, and its limbs moved restlessly from side to side.

They weren't alone anymore, and the creature seemed to realize that, too. It turned around, its attention on the darkness beyond. Aurora squinted past the spider, terrified it had some kind of mate that was coming to share Aurora as their dinner.

But then she felt it—the familiar slither of ice that coasted down her spine. A feeling she only got when Nyx was near.

Just as she gasped with realization, the spider shrieked. Her head spun as a heaviness pressed against her. Through the darkness, she thought she saw feathered wings unfurling before she blacked out entirely.

Twenty-One

Aurora

A cool breeze flowed across Aurora's face, gently waking her up. She felt weightless once more as awareness slowly returned to her body.

The first thing she realized was the cold chest her cheek was pressed to, along with the strong arms cradling her. She could still hear the soft patter of wings beating in the air, just as she had before she passed out.

She peeked an eye open, then the other, to find the world blurry around her.

Aurora's vision slowly cleared as she blinked several times, gaining her bearings with each flutter of her lashes.

There was no longer a terrifying spider shifter staring back at her, but the vastness of the night sky. Stars shone brighter than she had ever seen, so close she felt like she could touch them.

The brisk air sank its teeth into her skin, and she shivered. As soon as she did, the arms around her tightened, pulling her closer. She had almost forgotten about the arms—her mind was foggy and focused on floating in the stars.

Her gaze trailed up black cotton and paused at what she found beside her: great midnight-feathered wings. Identical to those of her raven. They glided in the air gracefully, moving in a soft back-and-forth pattern. They mesmerized her. Entranced her.

"Aurora," breathed a deep and familiar voice—perhaps the only voice she wanted to hear right now.

The wings were *Nyx's*...

She gasped and looked down to see the tops of trees so far below that she couldn't see the ground beneath their canopy of leaves.

"Aurora," he repeated, firmer this time.

She didn't want to look up at him, so she snapped her gaze to his wings. Where had they come from? How had he kept them hidden?

Nyx had saved her. *Again.* But she had doubted he would, and she was ashamed of that. Her life had a habit of turning into tragedy. Why would today be any different? He had saved her once, but how could she be so fortunate to be saved again?

His chest expanded as he sighed. She buried her face in his shirt, ignoring the cold that radiated off of him.

He flew them above puffy white clouds, so high that she could see the moon. It splashed hues of blue below, covering the ground.

As he lowered them toward a cloud, she finally grew brave enough to look at him. His eyes were already on her, his gaze darker than she had ever seen it. Both irises were black, a depthless void that captured her mind and spirit.

It wasn't until he released the cradle he held her in that she noticed they weren't moving anymore. His hand grazed down the expanse of her spine long after he let go.

The ground was supple, the stars still shining brightly beside them. Only when she looked down, she realized that they weren't on the ground at all, but standing on a cloud.

"How?" she gasped.

It was like her dream, but this time, it was real.

When she looked back up at him, the darkness in his eyes had given way to their usual soft navy and light green hues. He didn't answer her—didn't need to. He was the God of Fear and Dreams, the maker of Nocturna fae and wielder of the original shadows.

And he had saved her. Again.

His feathered wings stretched out and curved toward her, shielding her from the world.

"You have wings," she added. "And you're...here."

A small smile twitched at the corners of his mouth.

Aurora was still nestled against him, and his hands pressed lightly against her back as his arms encircled her waist. The way he held her was gentle—almost reverent.

"I didn't think you were going to come—or if you even *could* yet." Her voice was still breathless—from screaming in the cave, or from the awe of the flight, she wasn't sure. Possibly a mixture of both.

He nodded slowly and lifted his gaze above them. "You were in a place where I could not hear you, even in prayer." It looked as if it pained him to say this, his brows twitching together and mouth pressed into a thin line.

"If you couldn't hear me," she whispered, piecing it together, "then how did you find me?"

He swallowed, his eyes still fixed on the stars. "It isn't a matter of how." He looked down at her, their gazes colliding. "But when."

She opened her mouth, confusion swirling with the adrenaline that still coursed through her. He found her, even when he said she was in a place he couldn't reach her—as if they were connected, him and her. Two different beings bound together by an unknown fate.

For the first time, Aurora realized just how far Nyx was willing to go for her.

"I will always find you, Aurora," he said firmly. "Even the Goddess of Vengeance cannot hide you from me."

Her heart stuttered and began beating fast for a new reason. And that reason was staring back at her, waiting for her to say something—anything.

She feared asking what he meant by that—was afraid it meant something different to him than it did to her—so she settled on, "What does the Goddess of Vengeance have to do with this?"

His eyes flickered. "The creature that attacked you was a creature of hers."

She shivered, her body leaning into his.

"You're cold," he murmured. He rubbed his hands up and down her back, warming her. His wings pulled tighter around them, blocking the wind from hitting her face. But she wasn't cold—she had never felt more alive.

His hand crossed over her shoulder blade, where the rock tore into her skin. She hissed and flinched away. It was odd for the wound to still be bleeding—she should've healed by now.

"Did it hurt you?" His attention zeroed in on her shoulder, worry etched across his face. In the blink of an eye, he had her turned around, her back facing him.

"When it was dragging me to the cave," she whispered.

She couldn't see Nyx, but she could feel a wave of heat radiate off of him.

"Its web neutralizes your magic and ability to heal." His voice was tense. Rough. "Stay still while I mend it."

Aurora couldn't remember anything of what had happened in the cave past the sound of his wings before she blacked out. She didn't know if the creature was dead or still free to torment her village.

"So our village is safe now?"

He peeled back her shirt where it was torn, his fingers light. "Nothing is truly safe from Vidaris," he answered simply. "Not while she has control over the Vale."

Aurora almost asked more about what he meant, but something stopped her. She didn't know if she *wanted* to know so much about the gods. What good would it do her to know the terrible things that hid in the night?

"The creature is called a midnight weaver," he continued. "And she wasn't the only one. It belongs to a host, a group of twenty to thirty of them that nest close to one another."

Her breath caught in her throat. The village wasn't safe, then—Max, Leila, and Maliena weren't safe. Not when there were more of those *things* out there.

"That creature—the midnight weaver—that almost..." Her words trailed off, and fear gripped her chest. She could still feel its webs around her, pinning her arms down as she stared into its soulless eyes.

His fingers hit the sensitive flesh of the cut on her shoulder, and she flinched. He stilled, his exhale jagged. "Killed you?" he finished with a growl.

She nodded and said, "That one is gone?"

"It died screaming." His whisper was laced with venom, his emotions on full display. "Though not as slowly as I would've liked."

She stood in silence as he continued mending her wound. It caused a warm prickling sensation to spread down her arm and up her neck, itching like a thousand ant bites.

The stars twinkled around her, so she focused on them instead. It made her think of the dream she and Nyx had shared, when the clouds weren't real and only their spirits were present together.

Now they were truly *here*, standing among the stars and moon.

"It's better than the dream," she breathed. "Being up here with you like this."

His fingers paused on her shoulder. She felt him step closer, the ghost of his touch caressing every inch of her back.

"Anywhere is better with you." His voice had softened, his lips brushing against her ear. "You're a dream I never want to wake from."

Her blood hammered in her ears as her pulse picked up. The words floated across her heart and landed softly, embedding into her soul.

He had never been so blunt with her, and she was afraid that if she turned around, he would stop. And she *really* didn't want him to stop.

"For a moment, I thought I had lost you," he continued, his voice a deep rasp. "Your prayer was distant, as if you were yelling to me from a cellar and I was standing on the roof. I could feel your panic, but I couldn't pinpoint it."

Her body started to shake, the adrenaline wearing off and the realization of her near-death sinking in.

"But you still came," she whispered. "You always come."

He stilled behind her, his finger pausing on the small curve of her neck. "I do not wish to lose you, Aurora," he murmured. "I was prepared to kill anything in my path to get to you."

She twisted around, her body half-turned as she searched his face for any teasing. But his eyes looked hesitant, and, more than that... sincere.

Gone were the dark depths that had consumed his irises earlier. Instead, one shone a green so light it almost looked white—while the other was a pale blue.

"Why?" The question spilled from her lips as she held his gaze. "Why would you do that for me?"

His eyes sparkled—she had asked another question, but she didn't care about the deal anymore. She would tell him anything he asked of her.

"Because my heart beats for yours," he said softly. His eyes widened, as if he'd surprised himself by saying it. "Even if yours could not possibly beat for one as cold as mine."

She sucked in a sharp breath as the words slammed into her. Her adrenaline from being taken by the shifter had dimmed, but it returned with each syllable he spoke.

How did he not know there was so much of him to love? He was more than some benevolent being that sat high on his throne. He was more than a god, and as much as he may have liked to pretend otherwise, he cared for fae and humans alike. He was the one who had been there for her when no one else was.

Despite his attempt to hide that part of him, she could see through his façade—through the neutrality and uncaring aura he attempted to wear.

Perhaps she had always loved him, even before she knew him. But now, she was *in* love with him. Not with his power or his abilities, but his heart. It may not have beat like a fae's—goddess, she didn't even know if he *had* one—but she loved it all the same.

"I love every part of you," she whispered, terrified of scaring him away. Her heart pounded in her chest, thumping against her ribs with a ferocious beat. "The god of fear, the god of dreams—and everything in between."

His eyes widened, and his chest expanded as his breathing picked up. His wings squeezed in tightly toward his spine, tensing as he pulled them in. "Aurora—"

"You sent that raven to watch over me in the wood," she began, refusing to stop before he heard what she had to say. "You created a way for me to get to the Celestial Plane—to your home—just to stay safe. You stocked my wagon and didn't want anything in return. You saved me last winter, and *again* tonight."

He blinked silently but didn't deny it. She hadn't known if the raven was really his, but she had suspected.

"You've been visiting me in my dreams, despite saying you wouldn't see me again." She trudged ahead, not slowing down. "You care about fae and humans—"

"You're wrong," he interrupted, his voice a low hum. "I don't care about what fae or humans do. I don't care whether they live or die. And I certainly don't care that they call me a dark god and exile anyone who chooses to worship me."

Aurora was positive that the air was squeezed entirely from her lungs.

His eyes snapped back to a deep black, swirling with a blazing intensity. He leaned closer to her, a small sneer on his lip as if he wanted to frighten her.

But she wasn't afraid.

His hands slid onto her face, cupping her cheeks. He leaned closer, his gaze still burning as he said, "You are what I care about, Aurora."

His fingers plunged into her hair, tilting her face up to his.

When her lips met his, she felt the stars sing and the moon shout. It was a fire that consumed her, a heat that swallowed her whole.

Twenty-Two

Aurora

Aurora had been kissed before—just as she had been touched. But she had never been loved, not like this. Not in a way that made the world around her fade away into nothing, as if only the feel of Nyx's lips against hers existed.

She began unbuttoning his shirt, desperate for more, but he pulled back, breaking their kiss.

"If you want to take this slow—"

"That's the last thing I want," she said breathlessly. Adrenaline from her near-death experience still raged through her veins. "Unless that's what you want?"

His jaw clenched, and his fingers lazily moved to his shirt, unhooking the remaining buttons. "There is nothing I want more than you." He slipped his arms out of his shirt, which fell to the clouds at their feet.

She had never seen someone so beautiful—so hauntingly gorgeous. The ridges of his abdomen were sharp and perfect, as if carved from stone. His midnight hair was tossed across his face, making him look younger than...however old a god was.

His wings pressed together, slowly retreating into his back.

"Leave them," she blurted. He smirked, and her face reddened. "If this is you, I want every part of that."

His gaze softened, and he took a step toward her. "Turn around."

She did as he asked, facing away from him. His fingers started at the buttons at her neck, undoing them one by one until they reached her lower back.

Cool air licked down her spine. She heard a rustle, then felt his soft lips press to the top of her neck.

His hands glided down her waist, gripping her hips. Her body swayed back, leaning into his touch. Slowly, he kissed down the length of her back, taking the fabric of the dress with him and peeling it off of her.

When he pressed his lips, finally, against the lower curve of her spine, she felt his fingers tighten and dig into her hips. The fabric pooled at her waist, but he didn't seem in a hurry to remove it.

He spun her around to face him. She gasped softly when she found him on his knees, staring up at her. Slowly, he peeled off the rest of her gown, letting it slip to her feet.

She shivered as his fingers closed around her ankle. He hooked her foot over his shoulder, leaving her to balance on one leg while the other was draped over his back.

He turned his face toward her thigh, peppering her skin with kisses. Heat pooled low in her stomach and followed the path of his lips toward her center.

When his mouth closed over her, her hands shot forward to grip his hair. His wings stretched out behind him, rustling as he groaned into her.

She trembled as he spared her body no mercy, his tongue licking and mouth sucking. Her body writhed in his grasp while his hands gripped her hips to keep her still.

The stars around them blurred, her vision growing hazy as pressure built between her thighs. She could feel his tongue stroking her over and over again, while one of his hands released her hip.

She wiggled against him, desperate for more. He slowly slipped two fingers into her, working them in tandem with his tongue.

The feel of his fingers pumping in and out made her eyes cross, the pressure finally reaching a tipping point. When the stars fractured and her body pulsed with pleasure, she cried out. Every nerve ending was set aflame by his touch.

He leaned away, gently setting her foot back down and removing his hands from her body.

She watched as he unhooked his pants, slipping them off. Her mouth went dry as she looked at him. How could she possibly measure up to a god? One chiseled to perfection…

Sensing her hesitation, he stepped forward and put a finger beneath her chin. "You are the most stunning creature I have ever known." His words brought tears to her eyes. He leaned down, his face inches from hers. "I have never felt such fear as I did when I realized where you had been taken."

She stood on her toes, pressing a kiss to his mouth. His body responded instantly, pulling her in close. He lowered her down, setting her back against the top of the cloud. It was softer than any furred blanket, lighter than any feather.

He hovered over her, pausing to trace her face with his eyes. "Ask me a question," he breathed.

She tilted her head to the side, thrown off by his abrupt demand.

"Our deal is still in place," he added.

Realization swept through her, and she smiled. "Are you always so bossy?" She smirked.

A smile tugged at his lips. "Always," he said as he settled himself on top of her. The weight of him felt like bliss, but nothing could compare to the way his skin felt against hers. His body was firm and rigid, but still melted into hers, melding them together. He tucked a strand of hair behind her ear and left his fingers intertwined there. "My turn."

She had never been more thankful for the night she made that deal.

"Tell me what I can do to keep you." His eyes gleamed against the moonlight. "Because I've never loved someone how I love you, Aurora. Gods aren't meant to be with fae or humans. But I don't care what the Divine have decided upon. If the mortals of this plane consider me dark, then I'll be dark. I'll do what has to be done if it means keeping you."

She needed to feel him—needed to have him closer.

"You have me," she whispered. "Forever."

He slid into her, and they gasped in unison. His wings unfurled and spread out wide again, rustling with each thrust.

She was obsessed with the feel of him—intoxicated. And she never wanted to let go.

The clouds writhed beneath her, forming to the shape of her body and reaching up to graze her skin as if trying to pull her in deeper. Every wisp seemed to work in tandem with Nyx, caressing every untouched area of her flesh. When his hands left her hair, thin wisps replaced them.

Aurora moaned as tendrils of clouds gripped her hips, slipping between Nyx's fingers as he held his hands there too.

Her magic built inside of her. It needed an outlet.

"Let yourself feel," he whispered into the soft curve of her neck. "Be free."

His command was all it took.

She let her magic slip out from her hands, winding around their bodies and twisting into the clouds. The inky tendrils melded with the soft white wisps, drawing pleasure from not just her body, but also her soul.

Nyx's magic was eager to play with hers, shadows of his own flowing around hers. They grazed down her waist, brushing against her skin with sparks of energy. It was unlike anything she had ever felt.

Every inch of her body sparkled with electricity as tension built low in her stomach again. She was being touched *everywhere* all at once—from Nyx's hand gliding up her body and gently cradling her cheek to the wispy tendrils of clouds that pushed her body harder into his. It was overwhelming—exhilarating. Almost too much for her to stand.

The cloud beneath her raised, just enough to angle her hips higher, allowing Nyx to slip in deeper.

Her vision grew hazy again, and she lifted her eyes to the stars. Her back arched as Nyx drove into her.

"I am yours," he promised. "Now until the day you choose otherwise."

It was her undoing. Her damnation.

When she cried out, he followed her over the edge, holding her close as they fell into oblivion together.

Twenty-Three

Aurora

Aurora wasn't ready to return to her village—to say goodbye to Nyx. But she didn't want her siblings to wake without her being there. She wished she were returning knowing the monster that terrorized her village was slain, but they were all wrong. It wasn't a singular creature, but a whole host of midnight weavers—Vidaris's pets.

Nyx flew them as close to her cottage as he could. All the while, Aurora couldn't take her eyes off of him.

"When will I see you again?" she asked.

He smiled down at her as he began descending to the snowy forest floor. "Whenever you want to."

When her feet touched the ground, her head spun and her body swayed—as if her senses still thought they were flying.

A twig snapped behind them, and she jumped, twisting around.

Nyx smiled and nodded in the direction of the sound. "Just a winter fox."

Knowing that those *monsters* were lurking in the forest, waiting to take someone into their webs... It made it all the worse knowing it wasn't just one creature. They *had* to stop them.

"Nyx." She hesitated, struggling to find the words. He reached under her chin and lifted her face to his. Her eyes pleaded with him. She took a deep breath and said, "You have to help rid us of the midnight weavers. My siblings will never truly be safe."

His jaw clenched. "It isn't that simple."

"Then explain it to me so I can understand why," she begged. "You're...you! There has to be something—"

"No," he gritted out. His hand fell away from her chin at the same time his wings disappeared from behind him. "With Vidaris holding the seat of ruling the Vale, there is no winning. No hiding. One of her creatures going missing will go unnoticed, but if they *all* start dying... She's going to turn her eye to where they're disappearing from."

His words sank in.

"Meaning—" She swallowed. "She'll look here."

He nodded slowly, his gaze unreadable. "Give me some time to figure it out." He reached for her cheek, resting his palm gently against it. "Continue to stay out of the forest at night and call out to me the *moment* something feels off."

She didn't want to say goodbye, but as the sun neared the horizon, she knew it was time.

"I will," she promised.

With a soft kiss pressed to her lips, he disappeared into the sky as he so often did.

***

Aurora floated to the back of her cottage, the morning bright enough to see the outline of the wood storage shed. Her fingertips grazed the wooden slats as she walked around to the front.

She never imagined her life to be like this. Love had never been something she thought she'd have. But Nyx wasn't someone she could...marry. Blessed Divine, he was a *god*. She wouldn't be able to have a house with him in the village. They couldn't travel together. He couldn't meet her siblings.

The reality of their situation weighed on her now that she was alone. It wouldn't be easy, but they would figure it out.

When she pushed through the front door, she realized how exhausted she was—her body from fighting to get away from the midnight weaver, her soul for being laid so bare to Nyx. Muscles she hadn't felt before ached, and the ones beside those did too.

She just needed to rest a little; to let her body recoup and her mind fall into the blissful oblivion of sleep. After slipping off each boot and setting it by the fire to dry, she walked stiffly to her and Max's room.

As quietly as she could, she slipped into their bedroom. The floorboards beneath her groaned in protest, and she silently cursed them for being so loud. She glanced at Max's bed to see if he had woken up, but froze when her gaze landed.

The bed was empty.

He shouldn't have been gone yet—curfew remained in place until first light, which hadn't yet arrived. But he certainly wouldn't have left before she came into the cottage.

With trembling fingers, she pushed the door aside, no longer masking her footsteps as she made her way to Leila's room. She searched the dining area and kitchen in one fell swoop, finding it empty.

Leila will know where he's gone, she assured herself.

The walk was short, the cottage small enough that she arrived at her door in a few steps. She knocked twice, pausing to see if Leila was up. But the cottage was silent. Far too silent for her younger siblings, who were so full of life that it filled their worn-down home to the brim.

"Leila," she breathed as she pushed into her room.

Her little sister didn't answer. Aurora's eyes widened when she found her bed empty, too. She shook her head and backed out of the room, mumbling to herself the reasons they could be out of the cottage and where they would go.

They could've found me gone and went to Maliena's, she thought as she yanked her snow boots back on. *Or to a friend's house—*

A heartbreaking wail cried out in the distance, loud enough for Aurora to hear through her house. Her heart beat faster, and she hoped it was just a coincidence—simply bad timing to find her siblings out when they weren't supposed to be.

But her worry propelled her feet swiftly toward the cry, her knees trembling. It was coming from the center of their village—too loud to miss. An icy dread burned like a pit in her chest as she neared it.

There was a small crowd scattered around the square; more people than she would've expected to be out at first light.

Elara was standing in the middle, her arms stretched out as she talked. Aurora strained to hear what she was saying, but there was too much happening, the people around her talking over one another.

She spotted Maliena in the fray, her hands pressed to her stomach. Panic gripped Aurora's throat as she watched Maliena sob into her hands, her knees pressed into the mud. The wailing Aurora heard was Maliena—a pain so deep and raw that she didn't recognize it as coming from her oldest friend.

Aurora's body went numb, unable to feel the rocks she tripped over as she stumbled to Maliena.

"Mali?" Aurora whispered, her voice shaky.

Maliena's head snapped up. Her skin paled, and her shoulders shook.

"What's happened?" Aurora demanded.

But all Maliena could do was stare, her tears still flowing down her cheeks as Aurora got closer.

"Mali?" Aurora crouched down and gripped Maliena's shoulders, desperation taking hold.

Maliena reached out, the tips of her fingers hovering beside Aurora's cheek as if she were afraid of touching her. "You're alive," she rasped. "We thought it got you, too." She threw her arms around Aurora's shoulders, squeezing her close.

Aurora's heart sank. "'Too'?"

Maliena pulled back, and her face crumpled. Aurora left her hands resting gently on Maliena's shoulders, worried her friend would fall to the ground if she let go.

"Max disappeared last night. Taken by the monster," Maliena sobbed. "I tried to stop them, but they were so angry—so convinced it was her fault."

Her world slowed to a stop at those words. *Max taken. Her fault.*

Aurora shook her head and squeezed Maliena's shoulders tighter. "What are you saying?"

She didn't want to believe what she was hearing—refused to accept it as the truth. Max couldn't have been taken; he knew better than to go out after curfew.

Unless...

Unless he found her bed empty. Unless he heard the awful buzzing, too, and had stumbled into the wood to get away from it.

Maliena swallowed, then said, voice quiet, "The townspeople blamed Leila for you two being taken. They said they found her with a dark god tribute."

Max had been taken, and her sister had been blamed and cast out. Images flashed—Max trapped within the web of that monstrous creature—and burned through Aurora's mind like fire blazing through dry hay.

Aurora knew what it felt like to be there, to be before the thousand-eyed monster and feel helpless beneath its evil gaze. Max was feeling that terror, was experiencing the very thing Nyx saved Aurora from.

But Max didn't have the connection to a Divine like Aurora did.

You were in a place I could not see you, Nyx had said.

Dread pierced Aurora's chest as the horror of what this meant sank in. If Max were praying to the Divine for help, they wouldn't hear him. Nyx had confirmed that much.

And Leila...strong and gentle Leila. It was freezing out, and she wouldn't know how to find warmth or take care of herself for more than a few days. She would be lucky if she made it through the night...

Aurora hadn't been there to stop it—she *should've* been there for them.

"No," Aurora choked out.

This could be fixed—she would find a way to make it right. She would get Nyx to help her find Max and search for Leila in the meantime.

"Tell me which way Leila went."

Maliena's bottom lip wobbled.

"Mali, tell me," Aurora urged. "I'll make sure everyone understands she wasn't worshipping the dark gods—just tell me which way."

The people gathered in the square shuffled away from them, hushed whispers turning into overlapping babble.

"There was no other choice," a girl Max was friends with said from beside her.

"There's always a choice," someone hissed, too quietly for Aurora to make out who it was. "We made the wrong one."

"Enough," Elara snapped over the bickering voices. "The evidence was there."

Aurora narrowed her eyes at Elara, the very woman who had carved the traitor's symbol into Luca's forehead, branding him as an outcast.

"What are you talking about?" Aurora demanded.

Elara's jaw ticked, and she tossed something in Aurora's direction.

Aurora caught it, turning it over in her palm. Her veins iced over as she stared down at the little wooden carving. She had forgotten all about this one—different from the one Nyx had taken from her.

She'd made this one the night Nyx had saved her the night in the wood last winter. It wasn't whittled like the other one; it was just a simple square block with Nyx's symbol etched into it, the unmistakable star with a flame resting above it. What made matters worse was the inscription it bore: *"In dreams there is freedom, and in shadows there is hope."*

She assumed she had lost it, had worried for a full moon cycle that someone else had found it and was going to turn her in. But as one moon cycle turned into two, and then three, her worry slipped away.

Leila must've had it this whole time...

"The God of Fear and Dreams is not to be messed with." Elara lifted her head slightly, her lips pursed as she said, "The safety of our village always comes first."

"This is *your* doing," Maliena snarled to Elara with such ferocity it startled Aurora.

Aurora's gaze snapped back to Maliena, eyes pleading with her friend for an explanation. She had a sinking feeling deep in her chest that she already knew the answer.

Finally, Maliena turned to Aurora and said, "Leila was already dead by the time I heard the shouting. They didn't cast her out; they killed her."

Twenty-Four

Aurora

Aurora jumped to her feet quicker than Elara could blink. Her shadows shot out from her body at the same time, seeking an outlet.

Elara took a step back, her eyes widening. But she should've moved more than just a step.

Aurora couldn't think straight—all she knew was rage. Elara could've waited before jumping to conclusions, could've cast Leila out instead of making her an example to the town.

Restraint was something Aurora had always excelled in. But not today.

Her hand shot out, piercing Elara's chest as she pressed it through her skin—her shadows assisting to slice through her body like a knife. Aurora's hand wrapped around Elara's heart and yanked it out in a single breath.

Elara's lifeless body hit the ground before she realized Aurora's fury left no room for mercy.

People around them gasped, some grabbing their children and yanking them away from the square.

"Aurora!" Maliena shouted, scrambling to her feet.

But Aurora didn't answer. She was vibrating with rage and heartbreak. She stared down at Elara's body, with a hole where her heart should be. The heart that still rested in Aurora's palm.

She'd killed Elara—ripped the heart from her chest without a second thought.

Hot tears welled in her eyes, spilling down her cheeks as she stared at the still and bloodied organ. Drops of blood speckled the ground, tainting the snow crimson.

Her vision grew hazy and out of focus the longer she stared. People talked around her, but she couldn't make out what they were saying.

She had to get Leila and Max back. Elara...wasn't her priority. She didn't fear getting in trouble—this far away from the queen and king, fae responded to strength, and most would see Elara as being the weaker of the two.

"Aurora," Maliena snapped. "You need to get out of here. Now."

The blood dripped off the heart and onto the snow with a soft *drip, drip, drip.*

"You need to take a breather," Maliena tried again. "Maybe lie down for a while."

The blood was all Aurora could hear.

Drip.

Drip.

Drip.

Crimson mixing with pure white.

Aurora turned to Maliena, her limbs heavy and vision still blurred. "Where is Leila's body?"

She couldn't see Maliena's expression, could only feel the pity radiating off of her. But Max was still out there—he could still be alive.

"Buried beneath the sacred oak," Maliena answered as she gripped Aurora's wrist and pulled her away from the center of town—from Elara's body. Elara's heart tumbled to the ground, and Aurora was almost certain her heart went with it.

"Max," Aurora stammered. "We have to look for him."

She could still save him if the midnight weaver hadn't—

No. She wouldn't let herself consider the possibility of him being gone, too. There was only one person who could help her now.

She pulled away from Maliena and sprinted toward the lake. Maliena called after her, but Aurora was already gone.

As her boots pounded into the ground, memories of her family flashed through her mind. She swore she could hear Max laughing and see Leila rolling her eyes. A tear spilled down her cheek, and she slapped it away, her breath coming out in quick gasps as she ran faster.

Leila couldn't have been worshipping the dark gods—Aurora would've known. But if she had found the carving and kept it all this time, Aurora may never know the truth. What Aurora *did* know was that it belonged to *her*, not Leila.

And yet they'd blamed Leila for bringing darkness into the village.

Aurora's fingers shook, the tremble working its way through her entire body as pain and rage began to take over.

This was all Aurora's fault.

Her feet slipped across the icy lake as she skidded to a halt in the center.

Nyx, I need you, she screamed into the void of her mind. *Max has been taken and Leila—*

Her knees wobbled. *Leila was killed. We have to get Max back.*

The fog rolled onto the ice around her, wrapping her in a soft haze. Once she heard her raven and saw the small opening, she didn't hesitate to follow it.

Her feet carried her swiftly across the lake and then through the odd forest. Morning turned into night in the blink of an eye as she made it to Nyx's broken temple.

Only, it wasn't broken anymore—the cracks were gone, and the ivy was cleared away.

It wasn't perfect, the stone still dull as she raced up the stairs, the walls bare. But as she ran toward the room with the white flame, she found shattered windows had been made new. They had been restored to their former glory, the glass composed of an array of colors. The moonlight streamed in mosaic hues of crimson, emerald, and teal onto the floor.

The raven cawed, pivoting to the left and disappearing into the last doorway in the hall.

Aurora sprinted after it, her chest heaving. She found Nyx standing in front of the white flame, his brows pinched together as he stared into it.

"A weaver took Max." Aurora's voice shook breathlessly. "And Leila is—"

She choked on a sob and brought her hand to her mouth. Deep maroon caught her eye, still covering her fingers.

Elara's blood, staining Aurora's soul for the rest of her life. She quickly wiped it on her coat, desperate to get it off.

"Aurora," Nyx said evenly, his voice devoid of emotion as he looked up at her. "Max is gone."

She shook her head and looked back up at him. "You can save him—"

"It's too late for me to save him." His eyes were far darker than they had been the last time she saw him, like a storm had rolled in on a bright, sunny day. "I cannot bring back those that have already crossed into Caelum."

Aurora's throat constricted, making it difficult for her to breathe.

"No," she snapped. "He isn't dead. You can save him."

His eyes flickered, pain flashing across them like a shooting star streaming across the sky—there one moment and gone the next.

"Max is gone," he repeated, softer this time.

Her anger gave way to a flood of anguish, a pain so deep she felt as if she were drowning, no longer held afloat by the hope of saving Max. She couldn't have lost both of her siblings. She wouldn't accept that.

Trembles began in her hands before traveling through the rest of her body. Her legs gave out, her pain driving her to her knees.

Nyx's composure finally broke, and his arms were around her before she could touch the ground, moving in a way only a god could. He caught her, his arms steady and cold as he held her to his chest.

She couldn't stop the tears from flowing, couldn't stop the pain from taking over. Even Nyx's presence didn't stave off the agony she felt.

His hand cradled the back of her head, fingers twining with wild strands of hair. "I'm sorry, Aurora," he whispered into her hair.

She sniffled and looked up, angling her face toward his. "You have nothing to be sorry for."

He held her gaze for a moment, hesitating before his eyes drifted back to the white flame beside them. "This is my fault." His voice was rough, and he spoke with a conviction so raw it scared Aurora. "Vidaris must know my weakness now."

Aurora's lip wobbled. "Your weakness?"

He turned back to her and pulled her closer, their noses touching. "You," he whispered, pressing his forehead against hers. "You are my weakness. If Vidaris knows, she won't stop until she's taken you away from me."

He wiped away a tear that fell down her cheek.

"Why would you think Vidaris knows?" she asked quietly, her voice uneven.

Nyx pulled back and sighed—not at her, she realized. At something he had battled with far longer than she had been alive.

"We have been at odds for millennia," he explained. "Vidaris and I have never been on the same side, as the realm has often thought. We both want the same thing for different reasons. The only similarity between us is how willing we are to do anything to get what we want. Good or bad."

There was so much Aurora didn't know about Nyx—centuries upon centuries of history and memories. She wanted to know it all, and maybe one day she would, but right now she just wanted her family back.

"Then what are we to do?" she asked, her throat raw as she screamed it. She pulled at her hair, her fingernails sinking into her scalp and squeezing until she felt a prickle of blood run down her palm. "How do we stop the weavers? We have to make them pay for what they've done to Max and Leila. *I* want to make them suffer until they can't hurt anyone ever again."

Nyx untangled himself from Aurora, helping her to her feet. His expression grew distant again, as if creating a barrier between them with his gaze alone.

"You will do nothing," he insisted. "I will find a way, but I need you to be patient. I need you to not seek me out or pray to me while I do this."

"No." Panic twisted in Aurora's stomach. "I can help."

He cleared his throat and took a step back, leaving frost in his wake. "You cannot go to these places with me. I must do this alone."

Desperation clawed its way up her chest and into her throat. "But what if you need my blood?" she tried, begging to help in *any* way she could.

He shook his head, his gaze closed off. "I won't need any for quite some time. Trust me, it's better this way."

"Nyx—"

The flame beside them flared, burning brighter and reaching toward the tall ceiling.

"I will find you when it's over," he promised. "Do not search for me unless you are unsafe."

Aurora sucked in a sharp breath, her mouth hanging open as the words speared through her chest, leaving a gaping wound in their wake. She couldn't be alone, couldn't lose him after losing Max and Leila.

She shook her head wildly, desperately clinging to the hope that she could change his mind. She may not have been a god—not even a high-powered fae—but there had to be something she could do.

Leila had been blamed for something she didn't do, Max had been taken, and her parents had been gone for a decade. Why did Aurora deserve to be the last of her family alive? She didn't—she *knew* she didn't. Not more than Max, so bright and ready to explore the realm. Certainly not more than Leila, full of potential with the strength of her magic.

So no, she couldn't sit back and do nothing. Not when she was all that was left of her family.

"I will find you again," Nyx vowed.

Before she could stop him, a chill swept down her back—the rush of his power washing over her.

By the time she blinked and opened her eyes, she was standing back in the middle of the lake with Nyx nowhere to be found.

Twenty-Five

Aurora

Two full moons passed, with Aurora going back to the lake every midnight. She didn't care about the curfew, didn't have anyone to protect back at home. With her siblings gone, it felt as though her cottage was taunting her with memories of the past.

Her desperation kept her alive—her body a shell that felt nothing other than pain and rage. All she knew was a desire for revenge, a hunger to sate the agony that filled her. Maliena tried to console her, bringing her meals and inviting Aurora to stay with her, and Aurora leaned on her as much as she could, but all she felt was heartache.

She prayed to Nyx all day, sought him out in her dreams, and yelled into the night while waiting in the middle of Lac Noir for him to come. But he never did.

Where she once felt wonder when thinking about him, she now felt desperation. Obsession. He hadn't said how long he would be gone; would it be decades? A century? Her raven was gone too, the skies quiet and empty.

She tried to find more information on the midnight weavers, searching texts from the elders in town and going to the trade post to ask those passing through. No one had heard of them and gave her either a look of pity or one of annoyance when she brought it up. There was nothing about the weavers; it was as if they didn't exist to the realm.

Her mind fractured a little more each night she returned from the empty lake without an answer from Nyx. It was as if she had lost him, too. She hadn't known love before, but she was certain it wasn't supposed to feel like this.

Half of her heart hated him for leaving, while the other had so much love for him that she could think of nothing else. Going to the lake was like picking at a piece of skin around her fingernail. She needed Nyx—the only one who had ever truly been there for her.

As the moon reached its highest point, she slipped out of her cottage. The village was quiet, everyone locked away in their homes while she made her trek to the lake. Snow crunched beneath her boots, winter still holding on as the weeks passed.

When she got to the bank, she caught a glimpse of herself in the ice and didn't recognize the person before her. Her long, dark hair was disheveled, sticking out in all directions.

She had avoided her reflection for weeks now, knowing she would hate the eyes that stared back at her. Now she knew why Maliena looked more and more worried every time she saw her.

Aurora shook her head and stepped onto the lake, her feet dragging toward the center. When she had first started coming, her prayers were filled with anger—demanding Nyx to answer her. But they had grown weary. Tired.

Still, a tiny spark of hope would bubble to the surface every visit. He had said he would come back, and each night she wondered if it would be the night—though it never was.

Tonight was no different. That same hope was so quiet, she could barely hear it whispering for her to not give up. Still, it was there. She shook with anticipation, waiting for the fog he promised would always come when she needed it. But the lake was clear, the air bright with the full moon.

Nyx, she pleaded within the safety of her mind. *I don't know what I'm doing here anymore.*

It was the first time she had confessed it, and now that she had, the floodgates opened.

I need something—a sign to know you're still out there. Her prayer grew desperate, but she no longer cared. *I can't keep doing this.*

Agony ricocheted through her body, bouncing around her chest and burrowing into her heart where it had found its primary residence.

"Please," she choked out.

Suddenly, a sharp pain jabbed at her stomach, and her hands flew up to cover it. She hunched over, breathing heavily through her nose.

It almost felt as if...

Suddenly, fog swept onto the lake, surrounding Aurora and covering her world in a blanket of gray haze. She breathed a sigh of relief and waited for her raven.

He had finally come—he was finally going to give her answers.

But the longer she stood there, the more she panicked. She didn't know how much longer she could hold it together without falling apart.

The familiar icy chill caressed her back, creeping up her neck and causing her to shiver.

She spun around, her eyes landing on Nyx instantly. Her pulse quickened with excitement at seeing him, a smile working its way onto her mouth. They were cocooned in a pocket of fog, still on the lake, not in the Celestial Plane where Aurora thought they would meet.

Nyx's wings were gone, his face blank. Her grin dropped when she saw the look in his eyes. But his gaze wasn't on hers; it was downcast, focused on her stomach.

For the first time since knowing him, she saw fear marring his face.

Twenty-Six

Aurora

Aurora wanted to say something—anything. But as Nyx's expression shifted from fear to pain, all thoughts escaped her.

Snow began falling around them, sprinkling through the fog. She watched as flakes dotted his midnight hair and melted on his shoulders. Her head was in a haze. She was uncertain if he was real or a mirage her mind had created.

She reached out, her fingers grazing his cheek, and he flinched, his eyes snapping up to hers at the contact. His fingers grabbed her wrist, holding it in place against his cheek. She gasped, her eyes wide. His skin was cold and soft, just as it had always been, but he was stiff. Guarded.

"Aurora," he whispered. "You are with child."

"*What?*" she stammered.

Every question, thought, or word she'd planned to pose to him disappeared. Out of all the things she imagined this moment to be, this was not it. Her heart clenched, and her thoughts raced.

"How do you know?" she choked out.

He couldn't know—*she* didn't even know. She'd been tired often, grumpy too. But that seemed to be her baseline lately. It didn't mean...

"I can feel it." His eyes drifted back down to her stomach. She placed a hand over it, the kernel of hope in her chest blossoming. "It has a piece of me within you."

Disbelief swirled in her thoughts. Had she been given a chance to have a family?

She looked down, a hand over her belly—no swell or sign of pregnancy. Her cycle hadn't come, but it was often irregular with the poor conditions of the village.

Nyx stepped toward her, a wave of his magic thick in the air. He placed a finger under her chin and lifted it, making her meet his gaze.

No words passed between them—none needed to.

With the good news came a rush of questions. A child without a father was easy enough to cover up, but what sort of magic would the baby have when it was born? Would there be any indication of its ties to Nyx?

While she wanted the answer to be yes, her heart clenched at the thought of what that could mean.

"How do we keep it safe?" she asked. "The weavers—"

"Are being dealt with," he promised.

Though the disappearances hadn't stopped entirely, fewer and fewer villagers had gone missing since she last saw him. Aurora was already convinced it had been Nyx's doing, but now she wondered: at what cost?

Her eyes widened. "What did you do?"

His face remained neutral, but his eyes gave him away. A small shudder of pain flickered within them, their emerald and navy hues darkening.

"What had to be done," he said simply. He leaned closer and pressed a soft kiss to her lips.

She trembled beneath his touch; her need to be closer intensified. His kiss was too quick, as if he couldn't stand to do it, yet couldn't stop himself. It was a kiss that felt like goodbye.

"To keep the child safe," he murmured against her mouth, "this will be the last time I see you, my dear Aurora."

It was the words that poured salt into the open wound within her heart. After all they had been through, this couldn't be how things ended. After all she had *lost*, she refused to lose him, too. He didn't get to roll into her life like a stormy cloud on a warm, sunny day and leave once the rain began.

Couldn't he see how much she needed him?

She choked out a cry and tried to pull back, but his grip on her chin tightened.

"Do not mourn me, for we have created something the Divine did not plan," he continued. "For once, this was not written on the stars of fate. If Vidaris learns of what we have made, she will stop at nothing to make it hers."

Aurora slipped her hands onto his chest, gripping his shirt. He held her chin steady, his eyes blazing into hers.

Words escaped her, her head spinning with all that she had learned.

There was no need for revenge against the weavers now, no anger to unleash. She was having Nyx's child, and...he was saying goodbye. A painful inevitability that she had resigned herself to the moment they met.

But that was before she had fallen in love with him, before they'd created a child together. She would not let him go this time, not like before.

"I believe you owe me a truth," he rasped.

She choked out a soft cry as the tears flowed. "Only if you'll answer one last question," she whispered. He nodded, keeping her face close. "Will you promise to protect the child above all else?"

Above all else: above her, above his need to beat Vidaris in the cruel game of fate... The list went on, longer than Aurora could possibly name.

"Aurora—"

"Please," she begged.

He nodded, an almost imperceptible tilt of his chin. She breathed a sigh of relief, trusting him to follow through.

"My turn," he rasped. He leaned back slightly, taking in her face slowly. His eyes traced the slope of her nose to its tip, the curve of her lips, and the pinch of her brow. "In truth, can you forgive me for the pain I've caused in your life?"

His question pierced her soul. It was the most vulnerable she had seen him, his gaze wide as he awaited her response. She felt his hand glide up to cup her cheek, and she leaned into his touch.

The pain he had caused? She huffed a laugh to herself, thinking of the ways her life had been turned upside down in a matter of one winter. She had lost Max and Leila. She had watched her village be terrorized by the midnight weavers—had herself almost died by one of the monsters—and had known a heartache so deep she didn't want to leave her bed.

"It's true that there has been pain—more than I thought I could bear—of late," she began, her voice soft. "Some days, I didn't know if I would make it to the next."

His mouth tilted into a frown, thinking she was done speaking. He nodded, his gaze falling to the ground. But she wasn't finished.

"That pain didn't happen *because* of you," she said firmly. His eyes lifted back up to hers, a million questions in them. "It happened with you by my side, taking care of me and keeping me safe. I would've died more times than I can count, Nyx. And, more than that, you gave me love. You gave me *you*."

Nyx's frown deepened.

"And I will not accept being apart from you again, not this time," she continued. "Our child needs you—whatever magic he may possess, he's going to need you."

He clenched his jaw as her words sank in. Slowly, he leaned forward, pressing his lips to her forehead. "Thank you," he whispered against her skin. "For giving me what I never thought I would have."

He closed his eyes, his brows pulling together as he took a deep breath in. Snowflakes landed in his eyelashes, dusting them lightly.

With his eyes closed, he said, "Do not mourn me."

"No—"

But it was too late.

He was already gone.

***

The months passed, and the snow melted away into warm, sunny days.

Aurora didn't stop praying to Nyx. Villagers had mysteriously stopped disappearing since the night he had learned about the child. The midnight weavers had vanished.

The town settled into the belief that Leila had been the reason behind it all—that now that she was gone, they had saved the town. But Aurora knew the truth. This was Nyx's doing; the very god they cursed had saved them.

Still, the townspeople were growing more and more restless. Without any disappearances over the last few months, tension should have eased. But as time went on, people grew more paranoid. They were terrified of someone ruining their monster-less oasis. No chances were taken—no lives were spared.

Still, Aurora wasn't afraid of the wood, not even at the midnight hour. She carved into a tree while whispering hushed prayers to Nyx. Maliena often went with her—or sought her out, knowing where she would be—hoping to get her to stop before she was caught.

But nothing and no one would get her to stop.

With each passing full moon, her mind slipped further and further. Her obsession with showing her love for him was all that consumed her time. She dreamed of seeing Nyx again, of the day he would appear in the woods or on the lake.

The lake had melted into a clear, warm pool of water. She would stand on its edge, hoping to see a glimpse of fog or her raven, which she hadn't seen since the night Nyx said goodbye to her. She had told him she wouldn't accept him leaving, and she had stayed true to that.

Be it by death or by life, she knew they would one day meet again.

Twenty-Seven

Aurora

Aurora's screams filled her cottage. Candlelight flickered in the darkness, illuminating the room as Maliena encouraged her to keep going.

"I can see the babe's head!" Maliena shouted in excitement. "Another big push!"

Aurora's body was aflame, burning with a pain worse than anything she had ever felt. Her heart hammered in her chest, eager to get the baby out and hold it close.

Nyx had promised to keep it safe. Would he be here tonight?

It's coming, she prayed as she screamed again. *It'll be here soon.*

The door to the cottage burst open, and the nursemaid came running in with a warm bowl of water and fresh cloths.

"*No!*" Aurora said breathlessly.

The midwife couldn't be here—of all Divine-forsaken people in this town, she could *not* be here when the baby came. She, of all people, would know what to expect when the birth happened, would know the moment things weren't as they should have been.

If the midwife saw a magic that a newborn shouldn't possess...it would ruin everything. It would put Aurora's child's life at stake.

Aurora didn't know what sort of magic would surround the babe when it was born, or if Nyx's magic would make itself known. She was terrified of it coming out with wings like his, an impossible thing to hide if it were to happen.

"She was supposed to wait until after the baby came," Aurora sobbed to Maliena as quietly as she could. A wave of pain contracted her stomach, and she groaned through clenched teeth. "She can't—"

Another rush of pain cut off her words as the baby finally came. The cry that filled the deathly silent cottage made the pain Aurora had felt disappear.

"A boy," Maliena whispered, her voice uneven.

A wave of emotions swept through Aurora, stopping at her chest as the words settled in the air.

We have a son, Nyx.

Her body trembled as she fought to push herself up on her elbows. She looked at the midwife, whose eyes were on the baby, as she said, "Please, you must leave. Come back later—"

A line of shadows flowed from the baby to Aurora, just as magic did every time a fae child was born. If both of the child's parents had shadow magic, then that would be the magic that presented at the time of birth. If the parents were Woodland, then light would often show—or water if the babe was of Undine descent.

But this was no ordinary birth.

The room erupted into chaos, and the midwife gasped when the mass of shadows bounced around the room, frantically searching for a way out. It blanketed the entire room in a haze of darkness before finally breaking above the babe and splitting in two. One side dissolved into a shimmer of light, while the other line grew, then suddenly dropped, severed, bleeding shadows like a snake with its head cut off.

"What is this madness?" the midwife shrieked.

The shadows disappeared from around the babe abruptly, the magic dispersing around the room.

"A cursed child! Not blessed by Eurydice," the midwife hissed and backed out of the cottage. "Just like your sister with your web of darkness—a product of someone worshipping the Triad of Dark Gods."

No, no, no. It wasn't supposed to happen like this. Aurora was supposed to keep the truth hidden.

Nyx! she screamed into her mind. *They know about the baby.*

Maliena jumped to her feet, cradling the babe that Aurora had yet to catch a glimpse of. The midwife was shouting outside, screaming about a sign of darkness returning to their village.

"Save the baby, Mali," Aurora demanded, her voice breathless.

Maliena turned toward her, and Aurora saw two bright midnight eyes, set in a tiny face, staring back at her. Their child had the color of one of Nyx's eyes—the midnight one.

A tear rolled down her cheek as Maliena shook her head. "Get out of here, *now!*"

Maliena began to sob and said, "I won't leave you, Aurora."

Voices grew louder outside, shouting cries of anger and outrage. Fire flickered through small openings in the cottage walls, and metal clinked.

The door shuddered and was forced open. A man Aurora had known since birth stood there, his face marred with rage. His eyes landed on the baby, fury in his gaze.

"We will not have a child of evil in this realm!" he shouted from the doorway, torch in hand. "Burn the house!"

Maliena screamed and looked at Aurora.

Aurora tried to lift herself, but she slid back down, too weak to get out of bed. Maliena was going to have to leave her here.

"Go," Aurora pleaded. "And let him know his father will always hear his call."

Maliena hesitated, but the sound of fire crackling against wood set her into motion. She couldn't carry the babe *and* get Aurora out.

As smoke filled the cabin, a tear slid down Aurora's cheek. Maliena disappeared out the back, hopefully running far away from this wretched town.

Keep him safe, Aurora prayed to Nyx. *As you promised.*

And, just as she always knew it would, the fire finally claimed her.

Epilogue

Nyx

Screams erupted from homes. Fists beat on doors as they tried to escape. No matter how hard they tried, they wouldn't be making it through the night alive.

Nyx wasn't going to let them out.

He could feel each and every soul in the village—those present for Aurora's death and those who turned a blind eye to it. It was all the same, each of them as guilty as the last. But the guiltiest of all was just out of his reach.

Something had veiled Aurora's prayers to him—he *knew* she would've called out to him. He had heard every prayer since the last time he saw her, watched over every dream, cared for every breath.

Tonight was different, and the only one with enough power to silence Aurora's prayers was the Goddess of Vengeance herself. Vidaris had to have a hand in this, though he couldn't confirm it—nor could he let her know she had found his one weakness.

Not that it mattered. She had taken the one thing he cared about from this realm and carved it out of his cold, dark heart.

There was a moment when he had felt what it was like to love someone the way he always saw mortals loving—with reckless abandon and unbridled passion. And yet he had let it slip through his fingers, had let Vidaris win.

One day, he would kill her for it.

But there were bigger things at play, a larger scale that involved more than just Aurora.

So, for now, he fed his rage by burning the village that had burned her. Letting the flames take every life and carry them to the Vale to be tortured for eternity.

***

"Open your eyes for me, love." His voice was coarse and gravelly.

Her face was scrunched, her eyes refusing to open. She was confused—how could she not be? Her soul had just been snatched up while on its journey to the afterlife. But he couldn't let her go there. Not with Vidaris. Aurora didn't deserve that.

"Please, Aurora," he tried again. "For me."

He watched as her eyes slowly opened. Her beautifully pale blue eyes, still the color of the winter moon—the most bewitching sight he had ever seen from the day he first saw her to now. It was the color of hope, the color of agony. He was a god; he wasn't supposed to notice things like that.

And yet he did.

"Nyx?" she breathed.

Her voice was soft and sweet, so different from the strength he knew radiated from within her. She could somehow be as gentle as a butterfly landing while also as fierce as an unpredictable storm. He was thoroughly wrecked by her. Obsessed. Everything a god shouldn't be.

And yet he was.

"Where am I?"

She trembled, and he didn't hesitate to wrap his arms around her. Without meaning to, his wings unfurled and curled around the two of them, cocooning them in a pool of darkness, his feathers rustling in the breeze.

"You're safe," he whispered, careful not to startle her.

She gasped and pulled away, her haunting eyes frantic. "Our son—"

"Is safe," he finished quickly.

Her eyes dimmed, the panic slithering away. He knew she would be confused, likely piecing together the last thing she remembered.

"Maliena has taken him to a place where no one will know who he is or the origins of his magic."

That seemed to calm her down enough to listen. Nyx had never done this before; it was just as new to him as it was to her. But he had to do something.

"So he's..." Her broken voice trailed off, eyes switching between being present and vacant. As if her soul was teetering on the edge of a cliff with nothing on the other side.

He didn't know what happened to a soul when it didn't go where it was intended to go. The last thing he wanted to do was damn her to an eternity of misery floating in a depthless void.

He placed his hands on her shoulders and pulled her in close, his face inches from hers as he said, "Maliena will watch after him. He will not go without love."

Her eyelashes fluttered as she blinked. She nodded several times, as if his words were an anchor for sanity to grip onto.

"Where am I?" she asked tentatively, starting to sound more like herself.

"You will not hurt anymore," he attempted to explain. Only instead of nodding, her brows pulled tighter together, more confused than before. "Your body is ash in the wind, but your soul lives on."

The words stuck in his chest as he said them, burning as they forced their way out. He had been too late by the time he realized what was happening—images of her crying silently as her own village burned her alive stabbed at his thoughts.

They killed her—had tried to kill their son, too. If not for Maliena, they likely would have succeeded. The thought was like acid.

Nyx swallowed thickly and cupped Aurora's cheeks, needing to feel her. She looked up at him. Both of their gazes burned brighter than the North Star.

"Your soul was bound for the Vale, destined for an eternity of pain and torment," he continued, despite the wobble in her bottom lip. "I promised to keep you safe."

He didn't know if he was making any sense—actually, he was certain he was doing this all wrong.

"You are dead, Aurora," he finally said. "But your soul is tucked away in my dream realm—a place no monster, no god, and no other fae can get to unless I allow it. Fate may have taken you from your realm, but it cannot take you from this one."

He watched confusion sweep across her face, her mouth twisting to one side. She looked as if she couldn't process what he was saying, her eyes growing more panicked with each passing breath. There had to be something he could say to ground her, something to keep her from losing her mind entirely.

She had grown frantic these past few months—crazed, almost. A soul bound to a place it shouldn't be was no small thing, and if her mind was already fractured before death...

He could lose her to a void. A nothingness he knew little about.

Things were about to drastically change for the realm she had once belonged to. Vidaris's plans were finally coming to fruition. Her schemes of war and chaos were close to tearing the empire apart, and he had no doubt she would succeed. Especially now that he had pledged himself to aid her.

But he was good at playing the long game, too. He had plans of his own, and now that Aurora was safely tucked away in a place no one could harm her, he didn't care what he had to do to get what he wanted.

He blamed himself for what had happened to Aurora—more than he blamed Vidaris, if he were being honest. She had lost her entire family and, ultimately, her life.

One day, everyone who caused her pain would face twofold what they made her feel. His plans may have been in place centuries before he met Aurora, but he would make the time for avenging her death. That, he was sure of.

Aurora's lip wobbled, and her knees hit the ground before Nyx could blink. She fell before him, and he bent down in front of her, knee-to-knee. He didn't know what to say—how to help.

"You found a way to save me," she whispered. "For us to still be together."

Understanding rushed through his body like a tidal wave.

He placed a hand under her chin, dragging her up until she was standing in front of him.

"If anyone is to be kneeling here," he said slowly, his voice painfully even, "it should be me."

He watched as her chest expanded and her breath hitched, frozen as the words hung between them.

There was a realm's worth of weight on his shoulders as he knelt with her. If not for Aurora, Nyx didn't know where he'd be today—or where he might've ended up ten to a hundred years from now.

She had always prayed to him, prayed for his help and his grace. But she was wrong. Aurora was so much stronger than he was—he knew that now.

As a weighted silence stretched between them, he gathered the courage to say the one truth he had yet to admit.

"You saved *me*, my dear Aurora. It was never you that needed me, but I that needed you."

Aurora's gaze slowly lifted to meet his, and what he saw matched what stirred inside of him. It wasn't tenderness he found there, nor gentleness. Instead, her eyes *blazed*. Just as his heart burned for hers.

His lips parted as he sucked in a sharp breath. He found himself trapped within her stare, each of his limbs locked in place as he shivered beneath that look.

She was so quiet, so lost within her mind. He grasped for the only thing he could think of to tether her to this moment.

"I have a truth left," he said quietly, their knees still pressed together. "Several, actually, but there's only one I wish to know."

Her shoulders loosened, and she clung to every word. "A question for a truth," she murmured—almost chanted, like a prayer.

He smiled—or thought he was smiling; it was still hard to tell. The moment he had the idea of making this deal with her was the first time he had felt joy in a very long while. She had accepted it so eagerly, so trustingly—far more trusting than he deserved.

There was so much he had to say, but he had an eternity left with her now.

She waited patiently, her eyes wide as she waited for the truth he would ask of her. Nyx would never love another the way that he loved her.

"Well?" she prompted.

He reached for her, resting his palm against her cheek. She relaxed into him and slipped her hand over his.

"The truth is mine this time," he began. "I met a woman who was as beautiful inside as she was on the outside. Her bravery wasn't in her ability to fight or her skills of cunning; it was in her selflessness. Her courage to do what was right. And I will never leave her again."

Her lips parted, and tears gathered in her eyes. "That's not how the deal works," she choked out, her laughter stuttering as she swiped a tear away. "But I suppose we have forever now."

The sparkle in her gaze told him that her soul was more firmly planted in this realm now—in his dreams. And now, he had a new deal to uphold. A deal with the Goddess of Vengeance and the war that was about to break loose.

"What will become of our son?" Aurora whispered.

It was a question he had been avoiding. He could evade with half-truths when asked about his safety, but she'd thought to ask the one thing he had hoped she wouldn't.

Nyx's eyes met hers as he said, "The gods have plans for him and our line, dear Aurora."

After all, gods loved to make deals.

Dear Reader,

Thank you so much for reading *Midnight Tempest*. I would greatly appreciate you taking the time to review on Goodreads, Amazon, or social media. None of this would be possible without each and every reader, review, post on social media, or telling your friends and family about my books. From the bottom of my heart, thank you for choosing this book to read. Out of the never-ending TBR pile, you found this one!

Until next time,
Kara.

Kara Douglas

Join My Newsletter for updates & more!

www.karadouglasauthor.com

Social Media:
@authorkaradouglas

Books by Kara Douglas

The Unraveled Fate Series:

Luanria

Illuminance

Undying Lands

Coming soon: Ignite

Coming soon: Book Four

Acknowledgments

It's surreal to be finished with my next book. For those that have been with me since my debut, Lunaria, came out, thank you for being here. I can't thank you enough for helping me get to where I am today. I'm eternally thankful for your support, kindness, reviews, and support via social media. For the new readers, welcome! What an honor it is to have you here. I hope some part of this book spoke to you in a way that sticks with you. Thank you for being here and taking a chance on me.

To my beta readers, thank you for making this book into what it is today. I couldn't do this without your help. You have been a vital part in shaping this book into the final product—a product I can be proud of.

My girls, you know who you are. This wild rollercoaster of being an author wouldn't have been one I could stay on without you all. The sisterhood we've formed is one that I cling to on the hard days, and run to celebrate with on the good days. You have my endless thanks and love for being by my side all this time.

To my Virgo and Scorpio angels, I love you with all of my heart. You have kept me strong and supported for so long now. Thank you for always celebrating with me and filling me with deep love.

To my family, friends, and husband; thank you for your never-ending support of this journey the last few years. From late nights up writing, to weekends holed up in my office, you've been there every step of the way. I truly could not be here without each and every one of you.

With love,
Kara.